ELIMINATION

ELIMINATION

Ed Gorman

2 0 MAY 2016

Severn House

This first world edition published 2015
in Great Britain and the USA by
SEVERN HOUSE PUBLISHERS LTD of
19 Cedar Road, Sutton, Surrey, England, SM2 5DA.
Trade paperback edition first published 2015
in Great Britain and the USA by
SEVERN HOUSE PUBLISHERS LTD.

British Library Cataloguing in Publication Data

Gorman, Edward author.
  Elimination. – (The Dev Conrad series)
  1. Conrad, Dev (Fictitious character)–Fiction.
  2. Political consultants–United States–Fiction.
  3. Politicians–Assassination attempts–Fiction.
  4. Suspense fiction.
  I. Title II. Series
  813.5'4-dc23

ISBN-13: 978-0-7278-8466-4 (cased)
ISBN-13: 978-1-84751-595-7 (trade paper)
ISBN-13: 978-1-78010-646-5 (e-book)

Typeset by Palimpsest Book Production Ltd.,
Falkirk, Stirlingshire, Scotland.
Printed digitally in the USA.

To my longtime friend and agent, Dominick Abel

ACKNOWLEDGMENTS

Thank you to my sweet and hilarious first editor Linda Siebels, one of the finest people I've ever known.

Thanks to all the organizations dedicated to keeping all of us with the incurable cancer multiple myeloma alive as long as possible. Thank you, my friends.

*T*here was one of them that scared Dave.
The one who was always talking about Lee Harvey Oswald
and the guy who popped Martin Luther King.
What that would've been like.
The balls that would've taken.
Dave agreed with a lot of what the other ones talked about. How all the minorities got privileges the whites didn't. How the fags were making a mockery of normal life. How the things they were teaching in school were making gullible kids ashamed of their country and its history.
But actually assassinating somebody . . .
Cindy hated his friends enough already. If she ever heard them talking about that kind of thing . . .
So it was kind of funny that he would be the one the man with the money would approach. The man who wondered if he could interest Dave in doing a certain kind of job . . .

PART ONE

ONE

They're still out there.

'*You bitch. I hope somebody gives you a mastectomy the hard way.*'

'*I'm watching you. Every single day I watch you. I own about a hundred of those guns you're trying to take from patriots across this country.*'

'*God is planning to make an example of you for how you've forced homos on our families. He has promised me that you'll be dealt with within forty-eight hours.*'

When Timothy McVeigh detonated a truck bomb, killing 168 people and injuring more than 600, I remember thinking maybe this country will come to its senses again. Move back to the center. Get together again without all the acrimony.

I was wrong. The militia movement McVeigh had championed had grown stronger than ever. The rhetoric had become bizarre, then clinically insane. Not that I disagreed with everything the far right said. I consider the massacre at Waco and the murders at Ruby Ridge reprehensible. Waco is a crime of historical proportions. Many government people should have gone to prison. Needless to say, though I work for the liberal party I don't always agree with its conventional wisdom.

But what brought all this to mind were the emails I was reading on this rainy autumn afternoon in Danton, Illinois, population eighty thousand and home of Congresswoman Jessica Bradshaw, whose reelection campaign I was running. Her friends called her 'Jess,' and we'd begun to use that in some of our radio ads.

My name is Dev Conrad. I own Dev Conrad and Associates in Chicago, a political consulting firm. Previous to that I was in the army, serving as an investigator for several years. This election cycle my firm of fourteen people was running eight campaigns. We hired freelancers as we needed them.

I was in Danton because in the past three weeks we'd dropped three points in general polling and four in our own internals. We were now only one point ahead at best. The easy excuse was that our far-right opponent Trent Dorsey was reaping the rewards of having a fanatical billionaire uncle spending five times as much on TV attack ads as we were. I'd flown in early that morning from Chicago at the request of the congresswoman's chief staffer, Abby Malone.

'Uncle Ken,' as Dorsey always referred to him, had also hired a team of hit men who were experts at using automated phone calls – called robocalling – to smear opponents. You could reach thousands and thousands of voters this way in a single day. Robocalling became widely used after George W. Bush's people started the rumor that John McCain, their opponent, just might be the father of an illegitimate black child. The phone calls were particularly effective in the South.

This district was being bombarded by robocalling, suggesting everything from Jess as Commie, Jess as lesbian, Jess as drug addict, and that Jess's rich father had been mobbed up. Jess had won before because the man who'd held the seat ended up going to prison for taking bribes that unfortunately (for him) were videotaped by the state boys and girls. This time her run was different. We'd never faced a machine like Dorsey's and anti-incumbency was a formidable platform this time.

Danton itself was a river town that was heavily leveraged by a gambling casino. It had been known for decades as the place where Al Capone had sent his soldiers when the feds were getting ready to move on them. Not much had changed. The law, police and judges alike almost always ruled in favor of the gambling establishment. Jess Bradshaw's family had made their money in the stock market. They had not only survived the Depression, they had prospered from it. Everything was cheap, and if you had the money you could become unthinkably wealthy. Jess was an example of how wealthy. And she was typical of a Congress where sixty percent of its members were at least millionaires, if not much wealthier than that.

They're still out there.

'You have a lovely daughter. I wonder what her face will look like after I cut it up. One cut for every abortion you've made possible.'

'Fun, huh?'

Abby Malone had once worked directly for my shop in Chicago. At that time she'd been married to a young attorney everybody liked. She spent part of her time in Danton keeping Jess's constituency office running well and always preparing for the next election. Then one day she came into my office and announced she was getting divorced and would like to work for Jess directly. It would help her get over the end of her marriage. How could I say no? And having her there was probably a good idea anyway, even if it meant losing one of the finest employees I'd ever had, not to mention a world-class smart ass.

'I read them every day,' she said. 'I never tell Jess about them. If they're really bad I tell Ted. Some of them are so terrifying they're funny in a strange way.' In a simple red blouse and straight black skirt she was, to understate, compelling to see.

'Yeah, like those two morons in Florida who sent ricin to the White House a few months ago. One of them was an unemployed Elvis impersonator and the other a taekwondo dude who was running for president.'

Her smile parted the heavens. She was one of those slight, efficient blondes whose comeliness almost distracts from her skills as a planner and organizer.

'How's the prep going?'

Abby had spent the past four days in a rented dance studio firing questions at Jessica in preparation for tonight's televised debate. Given the polling numbers we were looking at, tonight's debate had become damned consequential. Jessica had to respond to and overcome all the lies Uncle Ken's money had been spreading for the last five months.

'She's good. So smart. I wish Ted was.' She allowed a wry smile for Jess's vainglorious husband. 'God, he's as narcissistic as a gigolo.'

'I guess I hadn't noticed that.'

'Yeah, right. You hadn't noticed. The old Dev Conrad deadpan. Cory told me he can't tell when you're joking sometimes.'

'The intern?'

'Yeah. He's good. I like having him drive me places. Makes me feel like a movie star.'

Cory Tucker was a political science major at Danton University. He was an amiable twenty-year-old who considered politics to be a cool and desirable calling. He also admitted that with so many young female volunteers it offered the possibilities of frequent hook-ups.

Then she said, 'Are you nervous about tonight?'

'Very.'

'Dorsey's an idiot but he does well onstage.' She checked the delicate silver watch on her delicate wrist. 'Hey, lunchtime. You really scared me when you said you were scared.'

'I didn't say I was scared. I said I was nervous. Big difference.'

'Well, whatever. So come on and have lunch with us.'

'"Us" being?'

'"Us" being me and Joel.'

'Well, it's tempting. I'm just so damned busy.'

'There's a very nice little restaurant about two blocks from here. And it's "Take an Old Dude to Lunch Week." I can find you a walker if you need one.'

'The arrogance of youth. I'm forty-three.'

'C'mon,' she said, that slash of a smile always preceding a cynical remark. 'You remember Joel. He's always got really interesting bad news for us.'

And so he did.

TWO

I'd seen family photos of them when they were young. Ted and Joel Bradshaw. There was no doubt they were brothers – they were virtual twins. And poor ones at that, growing up in a tiny white-frame house in New Hampshire, their mother working in a laundry and their father a philandering husband who stopped in occasionally between his benders and his shack jobs. But even then Ted stood tall and straight while Joel slouched. As a teenager Joel had been put in a psychiatric hospital for depression. The county had had to pick up the tab, he'd once told me, making his situation all the more humiliating.

I thought of the photographs as I saw him walk toward our booth.

He was an impeccable dresser, a man who preferred good suits and shirts and ties to any other kind of attire. And though he'd gotten even better looking as he'd gotten older, he walked with his head down and still had the slouch. I always feel sorry for the very obese ones, the crippled ones and the deformed ones who have to cross streets in full view of cars waiting for the light to change. Many of them keep their heads down. They know they're being judged and all too often found to be creatures of amusement or contempt.

'Here's a nice surprise. Great to see you, Dev. Sorry I'm late.'

'Hey, Joel, it's great to see you, too.' Abby overdid it but that temptation was always there with Joel. You just wanted him to feel better about himself. All the millions of assholes in the world and here was a decent if troubled man who couldn't seem to muster the least respect for himself.

He sat next to Abby and nodded to me. 'I'm sure glad you're in town, Dev. We really need help. I've been crunching all the numbers three times a day.'

He really did enjoy bad news. There was so little good news in his life, apparently, that his only succor was drawing energy from the bad.

I said, 'It's not over yet, Joel.' He always made me sound like a cheerleader.

To the waitress, he said, 'Steak sandwich and Diet Pepsi, please.'

'Dorsey's not a very good debater,' I said. 'I think Jess can turn everything around.'

'I've never seen her this scared before a debate and she's been in a lot of them. She knows what's on the line. It's never been this close before.'

And that was true. While Jess had never won with runaway numbers she'd always ended up with a two- or three-point win.

'Isn't Ted giving her his usual pep talk?'

Joel touched Abby's hand. Sometimes when I saw them together I wondered if Joel had a crush on her.

'He's trying. But it doesn't seem to be working. And I'm not sure he's giving her the right advice. He's back on the "maternal" kick again.'

'Great,' I said. 'Him and his "maternal" bit. He finally got us to try it in one debate last election cycle – she got pilloried by the press and we went down two points.'

'I love my brother but you know how he is when he gets an idea in his head. You really need to talk to Jess. Katherine flew in from college to be with her for good luck.' A wan expression came over his face as he said, 'Poor Katherine. I wish she'd meet somebody. She's always gotten these painful crushes on older men. I think she has a bit of a one on you now, Dev. Jess was always trying to get her interested in boys her own age. But instead she'd fall in love with the UPS guy or somebody who was working around the house.'

'That's sad,' Abby said, 'but maybe she's just compensating for neither of her folks being around very much. We thought of putting her on the campaign trail about five years ago but we could never be sure what she was going to say. That's when I got to be her sounding board. She was a really lonely kid.'

'I still think she could be an asset on the campaign trail.' The only time Joel sounded as if he had the right to speak was when he talked about working on his sister-in-law's campaign. In the D.C. office he was numero uno traffic manager. He had this ability to keep things moving. If somebody was a half hour late with a report Joel was standing at his desk. He had this enormous chart on his wall that he, along with most of the people in the office, called the Bible. He knew where everybody was for most of their twelve-hour days. What they were – or should be – doing. And if they needed him to stand at their desk or track them down by phone, so they could get their work done.

He'd had a failed marriage, two trips to rehab for alcoholism and several serious investments that had gone wrong. Ted's offer to work in the Washington office was seen by most people as an act of pity. But they were wrong. Few Congressional offices worked as smoothly and efficiently as Jess's office.

While Joel ate, the three of us gossiped about the latest D.C. rumors. Half of them were outright lies started by bitter enemies, but some of them were at least funny, especially a high-ranking congressman so fed up with the bathroom wait at a fancy party (apparently he was too drunk to realize there were two other bathrooms on the first floor of the mansion) that he pissed in a goldfish bowl.

It was always fun to hear Joel laugh. Even his eyes gleamed. The high drama and high silliness of Washington had given him his own world to play in. And find acceptance in. Even a few of the people on the other side – the ones who showered at least once a month and visited their dentists at least once a decade – admired and liked Joel. He'd also made a good number of friends through the Alcoholics Anonymous meetings that many Hill staffers attended. Joel went four times a week.

Abby said, 'You know they'll hit us with something at the debate. Have one of their questioners try to put Jess on the spot with something reprehensible.'

Joel said, 'Dorsey's people love hanging abortions on other candidates. In this district you've got almost a majority who are right-to-life.'

Abby said, 'They also like that three-way thing.'

'Wrong district. Won't work here. Very conservative voters. That's unthinkable to them. They wouldn't believe it.' He slipped out of the booth. 'Well, if I don't see you two before, I'll see you at the debate. Thanks again for coming out here for a couple of days, Dev.'

'My pleasure, Joel.'

After he'd gone, Abby said, 'I've always wanted to date a boy like him. Just, you know, out of curiosity.'

'What stopped you?'

'Are you kidding? I couldn't find any. I was in the wrong crowd.'

'The curse of being a cheerleader.'

'You'll never let me live that down, will you, Conrad?' But she'd started giggling.

'You're right,' I said. 'I never will.'

THREE

We'd heard rumors that men (and maybe women) with guns would show up that night to protest against the appearance of our congresswoman, who had apparently just returned from 'Islamia' where she'd learned how to implement Sharia law and had helped to plan the ultimate invasion of Islamists on the red, white and blue soil of the USA.

This was happening in all sections of the country; the gunslingers wanted to show off their hardware and their strange, perplexing views of our Constitution.

It was fully dark by six o'clock so the temperature was in the high thirties by the time the debate attendees showed up.

With my head still full of all the threatening emails I'd read, I stood outside the entrance of the university auditorium watching people come inside. The crowd was about what I expected.

In the old days the supporters of the other side would generally have been better dressed and more reserved. But such issues as abortion, gun rights, gay rights and education had changed the (if you'll forgive the jargon) psychographics.

Driven mostly by women, the shift to our side had been in process since the first Bush administration. This left the male vote heavily in favor of people like Dorsey, and you could see that in his supporters. Blue-collar and white-collar merged and their behavior was boisterous as they filed into the building and then into the auditorium.

But they were no less boisterous than the women and men on our side, who were hoping for an outright knockout.

There were six uniformed police officers bundled up in winter jackets and caps. Security was always heavy for these events. Some directed traffic as parking spaces began to disappear, while others walked the perimeter military style.

I didn't pay any particular attention to the old, tan-colored van. I saw it swing into the large parking lot and then be directed to a spot far down the line.

I went back to assessing the people walking inside the building. There was a lot of laughter, a lot of camaraderie, a lot of anticipation. A good old political debate, and it was encouraging to see that both sides had turned out so many people.

I heard the shouting before I was able to see, far down the wide central lane, what was going on. A pair of men toting AK-47s were walking fast toward the building. They were being pursued by another pair of men, these two happening to be police officers.

Let the drama begin.

The odds were greatly against the show-offs shooting anybody. What they wanted was to prove they had the right to bring guns of any kind anywhere they chose. This was the Second Amendment argument the gun nuts were always yapping about. They wanted attention and they would certainly get it. Within a few minutes some of the TV newspeople inside would hear about the confrontation outside and they would be out here with cameras and microphones making history. At least on the ten o'clock local news.

More officers joined in. Three of them stepped in front of the pair with the weapons and blocked their passage.

People were still parking and walking toward the door. But now they stopped and began to form a crowd. Not many of them looked happy about the weapons. They'd likely seen incidents like this on TV so pretty much knew the script – men and women with AK-47s were walking into chain restaurants. This had happened several times in our country lately. But seeing men with AK-47s on TV was different from seeing them only yards away. The TV people, maybe half a dozen of them, forced me to stand back as they bolted from the door as if the building was being engulfed in flames.

A gift from the gods.

An angry TV debate.

And guns!

The police had maneuvered the duo off to the side and even further down the wide lane. Three police officers dealt with them while the other three split up the crowd and waved it on to the building.

The conversation of those filing in had changed. It was no longer about their candidate or the debate. It was instead about the pair with the weapons. With one exception – a rather staid older man in a pinstriped suit and rimless eyeglasses – I didn't hear anybody defend the show-offs. He was talking about the Founding Fathers and how they would have approved making stands like this one. Apparently he'd been beamed down from the mother ship just in time for the debate.

I wish I had an explosive ending for this little tale. Fortunately, I don't. The cops, who handled it very well, quietly convinced the boys to save themselves and the taxpayers a lot of time and money by heading back to their van and going anywhere they chose – sans their weapons, which, even with the insane right-to-carry law in effect, were still illegal when displayed this way.

The duo complied. I was too far away to hear what was said but I knew there had been a few sharp words ('Constitution' could be heard several times). Then the tone started to sound downright civil.

The TV folks returning to the building moved much more slowly and looked much less alert than they had rushing out of the building. A few minutes of guys with big, frightening guns was all right but, hell, nobody had even pushed or shoved anyone. Damn. Maybe the anticlimactic ending made for bad TV, but as the night played out I would remember it as a portent.

FOUR

The modern TV debate requires the kind of schooling few candidates are prepared for. If it's done properly, the staff spends all available time pounding facts into their employer's head. Every possible issue, every useful piece of the opponent's backstory and several useful attack lines – hopefully ones that at least sting if not wound. All of these are put on cards so they can be studied over and over. There is also time spent on anecdotes that will indicate how concerned the candidate is about the common welfare. Other anecdotes are used to demonstrate how *unconcerned* your opponent is about the plight of average people.

Finally the campaign manager and the staff settle on two or three points that the candidate will make again and again in the course of the debate. Catchwords and catchphrases. If the voters remember nothing else they will hopefully remember these words and points.

Then, usually for the campaign manager comes the showbiz side of the debate. What kind of clothing, what kind of makeup, what kind of lighting. You have your makeup person, your speech coach and your personal TV dude. You can spend as long as a full day working on the stage where the debate will be held. You use a stand-in to make sure that you get every aspect of appearance and angle the way you need it. Earlier arguments would have resolved which reporters would be asking the questions.

The real wild card that night would be the audience questions. Fifteen minutes had been reserved for that. I had planted three voters – hopefully at least one of them would get through – ready and eager to humiliate Dorsey. Of course, he'd have his own plants ready and eager to ask Jess humiliating questions. For us this would be the wildest of wild-card moments. What had *their* oppo research rattlesnakes turned up on us?

I walked backstage. Rain dripped from my Burberry, so I tore it off and parked it on a chair next to a security guard, reasoning he'd watch over it for me. I asked him where I'd find Congresswoman Bradshaw and he said room four.

Backstage was crowded. As I worked my way toward Jess's room I saw two of Dorsey's people talking to a collection of reporters. They'd be telling the same kind of lies I usually did. Just earning their paychecks.

When I got to the dressing room I knocked and heard the unmistakable sound of Ted in full lecture mode.

'Honey, they want to see you *warm.* They want to see you *maternal.* That's where Dev and Abby are wrong—'

My knock interrupted him. Dev and Abby dumb; Ted brilliant.

A Washington columnist favorable to us once noted that 'lovely Congresswoman Bradshaw and her handsome husband Ted eschew the party scene, staying home to study issues their constituents are avid about.'

I would stand the columnist up against the wall and open fire for his use of 'eschew' and 'avid' and for telling the kind of lie Washington insiders would gloat over while they sipped their martinis.

In fact, the Bradshaws had to be dragged from the various balls and parties and 'dos' they attended four or five nights a week. She'd spent her summers in the Hamptons and studied for two years in Paris, where she'd done some modeling. He'd spent his teens and early twenties trying to fashion a professional tennis career for himself, but having failed that, he married Jess and took up the task of trying to fashion a political career for his wife. In addition to looks and money, they had what all politicians need: a neurotic – not to say psychotic – ambition to not only *stay* in office but to *advance* in office.

One more term in the House and Jess would announce for Senate.

I admired Jess more than liked her. She had that slight air of condescension all wealthy liberals have when they address the woes of average people, but her relentless battles fought for the poor and the helpless overcame it. She also had the same condescension for people she employed, including me and my staff.

Ted was a pain in the ass. They'd had two campaign managers previous to me and they both had the same problem – having Ted override their decisions. Jess had almost lost one election cycle because Ted insisted that they do things his way.

Ted loved being on TV. Some in the press (even the so-called 'liberal' press; if only they really were all that liberal) felt that the two had a Bill and Hillary Clinton problem. He was bright and shallow, known to stray from the marriage vows most folks attempt to honor. He'd always wondered why Bill Clinton had gotten in trouble over a simple blow job. 'What the hell? Who hasn't gotten a blow job here or there?' I assumed he never asked Jess this question.

In taking the job I'd made Jess honor a blood pact. Jess and I were the final authorities. If she sided too often with Ted, I would quit; if Ted went around me on an issue, I would quit; and if Ted had any contact with the press without prior agreement with me, I would quit.

I took care of his TV lust by having a media buyer in Chicago help me set up a half-hour TV show for Ted on Saturday afternoons. She got many sponsors because Ted would interview people on both sides of the aisle and talk about what the guests had done to improve the lives of people across the state. Sponsors loved it because it made them look patriotic and civic-minded, and Ted loved it because it was enough of a success to get him invited to Rotary Clubs and schools to speak.

As I was saying, my knock interrupted Ted telling Jess that my (and Abby's) idea was dumb and his, of course, was brilliant.

The room was small, holding only a makeup table complete with a mirror encircled with some electric bulbs and a counter packed with mysterious items for beauty, three wooden chairs and a movable metal rack holding empty hangers.

'I'd say she looks pretty damned good,' Ted said.

'How're you feeling, Jess?'

'Oh, not bad, Dev. I just hope I don't fuck up. I'm really nervous about this.'

'Oh, honey, you're not going to fuck up. Tell her, Dev; tell her she's not going to fuck up.'

I said, without smiling, 'Did you hear that, Jess? Ted said you're not going to fuck up. That's good enough for me.'

They loved their jousting.

'Dev, would you please tell Ted for me he's an idiot?'

'Just remember, honey, *maternal*. That way you'll get the "lady" vote.'

Ah, yes, the much sought-after 'lady' vote. I had tried, Abby had tried and Jess herself had tried to convince Ted that in this era voters wanted strong female candidates. They didn't care if the candidate was good in bed or even good in the kitchen. Women were the equal of men in this arena (personally, I would have been happier if the Congress was sixty percent women) and voters wanted women who exemplified strength.

'I'm doing this for your sake, honey.'

What happened next was one of those moments you never forget. Years later it would come back to me and still have impact.

Their daughter, Katherine, was sitting on a folding chair in a corner. She was the image of her mother, that indelible a match right down to the freckles across the perfect nose.

She was wearing a brown dress that made her all the more slender. Low heels and carefully brushed blonde hair completed her conservative look. She knew how to dress for her mother's public. She'd been very sick for a time and was still pale.

She said, 'Just be strong, Mom. Stand up to him every time he lies.'

And that was when Ted turned on her. 'Since when did you start giving your mother advice? Everything you tell her is wrong. You should be out there with the rest of the crowd. In fact, get the hell out of here right now!'

I suppose her 'be strong' suggestion went against his 'be maternal' idea, but there was a hysteria in his voice that was chilling. Ted had once slapped a male staffer. He did not like to be told he was wrong.

But Katherine was his daughter. And she sure hadn't deserved his rage.

'Oh, honey, don't get so worked up. It's not good for you,' Jess said.

'I know. I'm just worried about the polls, Jess. That's all.'

This startled me. Shouldn't she have been soothing Katherine? And shouldn't he be *apologizing* to Katherine?

But all Jess said was, 'Don't be upset with your dad, Katherine. You know how overwrought he can get.'

Katherine wasn't as hurt as I thought she should be, either. 'Oh, I'm used to it. If I got upset every time he yelled at me, I wouldn't have time for anything else. I just wish he'd take Xanax the way you and I do.'

'Well, I need to get going.'

Ted strode to Jess and kissed her on the cheek. Then he went to the door and was gone.

It was a full minute before anybody spoke once he was gone.

'Poor Dad. I feel so sorry for him.'

'Yes, honey, so do I.' Jess kissed Katherine's forehead.

Apparently it was me, not them. This was the way you treated your daughters these days.

FIVE

What we were about to see was the civilized equivalent of a prize fight. There wouldn't be any blood but there would no doubt be injuries. And while neither fighter would end up in the hospital, one of them might end up doomed to looking back on this night forever. Going over and over it, reliving with exquisite pain all the ways they'd humiliated themselves and lost the election.

The stage was filled with hurrying, scurrying TV techs checking sound and lighting. I turned around to get a look at the imposing auditorium. Lots of laughter and hellos and good lucks as the crowds chose their preferred side of the aisle. About half of them were in stylish attire for men and women alike. Again, like a prize fight.

Abby, Ted, Joel, Katherine and I sat next to each other in the front row on our side of the auditorium.

There was applause as the two candidates walked onstage. Jess waved and smiled. She took up her position behind the podium.

Trent Dorsey wore a dark suit with a white shirt and a red power tie. The grin that was always close to a sneer was firmly in place as he situated himself behind his own podium.

A middle-aged woman from the Voters' League walked to center stage and, much like a referee, gave us a quick lesson in proper behavior for TV debates.

Then the three reporters filed onstage and took their seats behind a desk. I was familiar with all of them. A conservative, a liberal and a young woman who seemed to be an actual independent thinker.

The fun started.

Judged by boxing standards, I had to give the first twenty minutes of the sixty-minute debate to Dorsey. He was his usual bellicose – read asshole – self.

He played all his greatest hits.

'It's time all the real patriots in this country take our country back.' . . . 'Have you ever wondered how many people in Congress actually go to church on Sunday?' . . . 'Are you comfortable knowing that homosexuals are teaching in our public schools?' . . . 'Now the government is running our healthcare system, more teenage girls than ever are getting pregnant. But it doesn't matter because they can just get a free government abortion.' . . . 'Wouldn't you like to wipe that superior smirk off the face of liberals when they're talking about people who own a lot of guns?'

He was skillful enough to twist any question he was asked into a mini-rant about his idea of taking the government back.

But at the twenty-four-minute mark – I was keeping close time – he made his first mistake. Asked about how he could support yet another tax cut if he wanted to balance the budget, he said, 'Right now there are men and women out there who are planning to make this country ours again.'

'Are you advocating armed insurrection?'

'I'm advocating driving the criminals and treasonists out of D.C.'

'You've spoken to several militia groups who seem to believe in armed revolution.'

'That's your interpretation, not mine. I'll speak to any group that loves this country as much as I do.'

He was shrewd but it was too late for that. In an off-year election such as this one the opposition generally took many more seats than the president's side. Dorsey had muted himself in the past three weeks and, coupled with the millions being poured into TV by his uncle, had caught up with us. But that night his vague response to the question about the militia groups capping his entire greatest-hit routine suddenly sounded threatening. He brought the old doubts about his wisdom back into focus.

The second twenty minutes were all Jess. She sounded sane, judicious and full of the kind of quick detail that impresses the electorate.

Dorsey stumbled. He started using words like 'responsible' and 'cooperative' and phrases such as 'the common good.'

The third twenty minutes was a fifteen-minute triumph for Jess, but right in the middle of it Dorsey had a good five-minute stretch attacking her for some of her more controversial votes – controversial in this age of plutocrats. Money for science, education and cancer research could be made to sound wasteful and Dorsey did a fine job of making them all sound like that. Jess was able to wrest back the lead by saying that she had an aunt at the Mayo Clinic right now suffering from breast cancer and she was glad she'd cast the Obamacare vote. She asked if there was a single person in the audience who had not been touched by the cancer of a loved one, and not just once but at least two or three times. I think a few of the people on his side of the aisle wanted to join the standing ovation our side gave her. She'd slashed his throat and he spent the last few minutes writhing in death.

Then came the questions from the audience. Predictably, the plants for both sides did their sleazy best. Boiled down, the questions were either 'Are you still having sex with the family dog/cat?' or 'If you had a chance to renounce your Russian citizenship, would you do it?'

They were too predictable, in fact. A fair share of the audience was starting to leave. I saw it as a pretty easy slog for both Jess and Dorsey. He managed to turn aside our bombshell question with an armada of anti-media and patriotic rants that won hearty applause from his side and some actual boos from ours. The son of a bitch never managed to answer a question straight on; in boxing that was called slipping a punch. In politics that was called making your case.

Dorsey's four previous questioners, despite the fact that they weren't naked and hadn't once mentioned Sasquatch, still had about them the faint stench of fanaticism. Two of them had glassy-eyed grins on their faces when they asked their questions, as if their queries would leave Jess gibbering and resigning. One of the other two wore a red, white and blue lapel pin large enough to serve a pizza on. And the fourth turned and gave two thumbs up to the stage before he stepped to the microphone.

But the good one, the one Dorsey had saved for the real shiv in the belly, was as upper-middle-class presentable as the woman from the Voters' League itself. Maybe mid-fifties, gray-blonde chignon, gray Armani suit and impeccably patrician face and poise. There was even a touch of Jackie O in her voice.

'Congresswoman Bradshaw, since you are so actively pro-choice I feel it's fair to ask if you, personally, have ever had an abortion?'

Jess handled the question with simple and believable grace. 'I'm not an advocate for abortion as some people claim. I'm merely saying that girls and women should have the choice of how to deal with their bodies. And no, I have not personally ever had an abortion.'

A cool, convincing answer. A quick survey of the panel's faces told me that they agreed with my assessment.

'You've *really* never—?' the woman jabbed again.

But halfway through her question they cut her mike.

This part of the evening had finished.

SIX

I headed immediately for the bullshit room, as it is so fondly called by operatives and press alike.

Adjacent to the auditorium was a small room filled with fine arts of various kinds. This would be used for more personal events. Right now maybe as many as thirty reporters and twenty camera people packed the place. The one absolute law governing the aftermath of a debate is that your man or woman, no matter how much evidence there is to the contrary, won the debate. Pounded the opponent into dust. Clearly entranced the audience and confiscated the vote of every man and woman in the auditorium.

But we really had won, so all I had to do was brag. Well, I had to tell at least a few lies to earn my keep.

Reporters, especially the TV type, love tabloid journalism. Slash, disembowel. But tonight they had to know that we'd won without much trouble.

'How're you feeling, Conrad?'

'As if I could go ten rounds with the world champion.'

'The world champion of what?'

'You name it.'

Polite smiles.

'What did you think of Dorsey's performance?'

'Which part? Canceling cancer research? Loyalty oaths? Or advocating violent overthrow?'

'You're accusing him of advocating armed revolution?'

'I don't have to accuse him of anything. It was implied in everything he said.'

'Think tonight'll help you in the polls?'

'Absolutely. The congresswoman was at her best and Dorsey was at his worst. I'm surprised his campaign manager hasn't attempted suicide by now.' Realizing I sounded too arrogant, I said, 'It's simple. Jess is the serious candidate here. She has a vital interest in making government better and that means saving the parts that work and getting rid of the parts that don't. But you have to do this carefully, intelligently. The well-being of millions of people is at stake every time a major policy change is made. That's why you want a person who has respect for her job. Serious respect.'

On the other side of the room there were cheers as Trent Dorsey held his clenched hands up in the air the way a winning boxer does. He was following the number-one law of the bullshit room – despite all evidence to the contrary. He was proclaiming himself the winner.

Over the next fifteen minutes the questions changed as a few of the right-wing bloggers drifted over here. They'd undoubtedly been using their questions to promote Dorsey's agenda. They'd saved their venom for us.

'There've been rumors in the past that Congresswoman Bradshaw has had a long-standing drinking problem. Is that what we were seeing tonight?'

'There've also been rumors that she's had a prescription pill problem. Was that her problem tonight?'

'Do you think we'll hear more about Congresswoman Bradshaw's abortion?'

I almost grabbed the little prick. All three of them were little pricks – three slight, dishwater-blond college-age boys in white shirts, blue blazers and gray slacks; the uniform of the salvation teams that come to your door to save your soul and annoy the shit out of you. Each blazer bore the crest of the local right-wing Christian college, Holy Shit University as I called all of them. They wanted our country turned into a theocracy. I devoutly did not.

These three were here to aggravate me into handing them a news story. BRADSHAW MANAGER ASSAULTS HOLY SHIT REPORTER.

Abby, who had been a little late getting here, grabbed my arm with surprising force and stepped forward to face the clone who'd asked the last question. It was a much prettier face than mine to put in his face and, because of that, more intimidating. All I could do was maybe throw him around a little.

'You came over here to make trouble. Go back to Dorsey's side,' Abby said.

'We have a right to ask questions.'

'Really? Do you work on the school paper? Or ever taken a journalism course?'

The clone actually blushed. But he managed to say, 'We serve the Lord in other ways.'

His fellow clones nodded.

'Then you're not reporters. You're troublemakers.'

The first clone took a step forward. 'We're here to expose the congresswoman for the demonic forces she represents in Washington.'

The second clone said, 'She's one herself.'

I was waiting for their eyes to start glowing the way the Devil-inclined do in horror movie posters.

I'd calmed down sufficiently to do to Abby what she'd done to me: take her by the arm. We'd been in the room forty minutes and the important reporters were starting to make their way to the nearest bars. There was no point in staying here.

We walked out.

Abby said, 'This is one of the happiest nights of my life. We did so damned well.'

'I don't know about you,' I said, 'but I need several hundred drinks.'

'Me, too,' Abby said. 'There's a place called Drink Up about two miles north of here. It's a decent place to get hammered.'

'How about if I meet you there in twenty minutes or so? I'm going to the dressing room to check on Jess.'

'Great,' Abby said. 'See you soon.'

She pirouetted, then skipped for maybe five yards and then shouted over her shoulder, 'We're going to kick ass, Dev!'

Laughter and the pop of a champagne cork.

I knocked and peeked in.

Jess sprang from her seat in front of the mirror and came over to me with her arms extended for a hug. Over her shoulder I could see Ted with a champagne bottle and a grin. Katherine was standing beside him.

'I was so worried I thought I was going to faint at times.'

'May I have some, Dad?'

He hesitated. Then, to Jess, 'You think it's all right, honey?'

'She'll be fine, Ted,' Jess said.

They were a family again – supposedly, anyway.

But obviously one of Dorsey's questioners had gotten to Jess. With a frown – she had been embarrassed by the attack and was not in a forgiving mood – she said, 'I did not have an abortion.'

'Oh, Mom,' Katherine said. 'We know you didn't. And even if you had, so what?'

'Hey, Jess, we're supposed to be celebrating tonight, remember?' Ted was master of ceremonies again.

Jess toasted him with what remained of the champagne in her glass.

'That's right, we're celebrating,' Katherine said. But the brightness in her eyes and voice had gone.

I listened for five more minutes but didn't really hear; I talked for a few minutes but probably didn't make much sense. I just wanted to leave and join Abby.

Then I was outside in the cold autumn night, the shadows hiding the assassin who waited, not for me, but for Jess.

SEVEN

The bar was a small neighborhood place with country songs and one of those female pub owners Graham Greene had once described as having 'a great public heart.' When she said, 'Nice to meet you,' you had the feeling she actually meant it. Her name was Mae Tomlin. She wore a Chicago Cubs T-shirt and a welcoming smile. I told her I was with the Bradshaw campaign. She said she was on Jess's side.

I joined Abby in a booth.

'Whew and double whew.' She drew a small hand across her brow and said, 'And whew again.'

'Indeed.'

'I'd say Dorsey is one unhappy guy about now.'

'Most likely.'

'Does that make you happy?'

'Of course.'

'Me, too. I know he's got a terrible temper. He's probably taking it out on his whole staff.' She sipped her wine. 'I don't know what Jess would've done if she'd lost tonight. I have to say she's not holding up very well this time around.'

'This is the tightest race she's ever had.'

'I know. I guess I never realized how much being in Congress means to her.'

'The big thing is she got through it.'

'Did you see Joel writhing in his chair?'

'He always writhes. It's like he's a little kid in a theater with a horror movie on the screen. He does everything except slap his hands over his face.'

'Every time she paused or seemed even a little bit rattled I thought he might get up and run out of the theater.'

Over the next few drinks I got her up to speed on most of the gossip in our Chicago shop. She loved the breaking news about two affairs and was sad when she heard that one of her favorite older operatives was retiring because his diabetes was taking his vision.

I was about to order another round when I happened to glance at the bar and noticed Mae holding her cell phone to one ear and sticking a finger in the other so she could hear above the jukebox. Then she jerked the finger from her ear and waved me over.

She slapped her cell phone down and shouted to a man standing next to the jukebox. 'Unplug it, Al.'

'Are you serious?' he shouted back.

'Damn straight I'm serious. Now unplug it.'

Not exactly a big job. The man pushed the jukebox away from the wall, leaned down and pulled the plug from the socket.

The abrupt end to the music startled enough people that Mae didn't have to shout for attention anymore.

Her eyes addressed mine before the other customers. 'My brother just called. He's still at the university. He said that somebody tried to assassinate Congresswoman Bradshaw when she was leaving the debate tonight. That's all he knows for sure at this point.'

Abby and I were out of the booth and half running for the door. I was saying the dirtiest words I could think of under my breath. Some of those emails I'd read this morning flashed into my mind as I got the car started.

One of those haters or somebody very much like them had delivered the ultimate message tonight. They really did want to take over the country by any means necessary.

Flashing red emergency lights wounded the chilly, cloudy night sky – two patrol cars and three unmarked police cars, a boxy ambulance and a fire chief's red sedan, though why it was here I didn't know.

The press was being kept a hundred yards or so from the rear doors of the building by a sizable cop in his uniform blue winter jacket. By morning the national press would add to the melee. After the attempted assassination of Congresswoman Gabby Giffords – though she had survived, six had died and thirteen others had been wounded – this would be more evidence that we were truly a gun-crazed country. The foreign press would love it especially. Unfortunately, good and sane people really could make the argument that we had become one of the most violence-crazed countries in the world.

On the way here the radio had informed us that Jess had not been hurt, nor had anyone else. The shooter had escaped.

We had to park even further back than the press. Yellow crime-scene tape had cordoned off a large portion of the parking area. By now well-wishers and zombie hunters had arrived; the first to re-assure themselves that she was fine and to pay tribute, and the second to wish that she'd really been killed – for political reasons or just because they liked the idea of somebody getting murdered. A near miss was better than nothing.

The night now smelled of cigarette smoke, gasoline from idling engines and a strong hint of winter. Near the doors I saw Ted talking to a group of reporters. For once his drama queen style was probably appropriate.

I hadn't had time to emotionally confront what had happened here. The only thought I had now was about the hunt – finding the bastard who'd tried to kill Jess.

The first cop I saw, I asked, 'Any idea where Congresswoman Bradshaw is?'

Suspicion, of course. 'And you'd be who?'

'Her campaign manager.'

'You have proof of that?'

I took out my wallet and showed him.

'He's really the campaign manager,' Abby said.

'All this proves is that he's really this Dev Michael Conrad.'

'I just want to know if she's been taken off the premises here.'

'No, she hasn't.'

He walked away and we walked on.

'What an asshole,' Abby said. Her rage was matched by her sorrow – her voice was trembling. She was much closer to Jess than I was. All I could think of was killing whoever had taken a shot at her.

'Just doing his job.'

'Oh, right, I forgot you were a cop once. At least, sort of. And you guys stick together. The thin black line.'

'Blue.'

'Oh. Right. "Blue."'

Abby stopped to talk to a reporter she knew; I walked toward Ted.

Five uniformed men and women were working a wide area with flashlights and evidence bags. Two others were on the roof of a large black storage shed. The shooter might have fired from there.

For the next fifteen minutes I walked around. I overheard policemen, average people, reporters. Every once in a while you hear useful things this way. In my army days I'd worked briefly out of Honolulu, where a man who'd been an informant for us had been stabbed to death on the beach at night. I'd been following him but was waylaid by a major traffic accident. By the time I got there, he was dead. But there'd been a party on that section of beach that night so I'd walked around, listening to people talk. A young woman had complained to her friend that a man had practically knocked her down as she was leaving the restroom and her shoulder hurt badly. I'd got his description and we were able to find the killer two days later.

No such luck tonight.

I was thinking of checking out the front of the building – I was told that donuts and coffee were being offered there, which sounded good on a night when you could see your breath – when I saw Ted begin to hold up his arms, signaling that he was done. I was close enough that he was able to see me. He marched triple time in my direction, trailing reporters the way poor children trail rich American tourists in Latin American countries.

'Where can we go?' He was moving fast enough that, despite the temperature, there was a sheen of sweat on his face.

'Front of the building.'

Then we were walking triple time together. We could have moved even faster if we weren't wearing topcoats. The reporters following us aimed their microphones at us as if they could actually pick up our words – we weren't even speaking.

Then, as we rushed along the side of the building, Ted said, 'Katherine's back in the dressing room with Jess. I told her to give Jess two Xanax. I need to talk to the press.'

He didn't 'need' to. He wanted to. The spotlight beckoned.

As many as fifty people huddled in the lobby. The aroma of hot fresh coffee welcomed us.

The ghosts of modern assassinations roamed the halls of the building tonight. Jack and Bobby Kennedy and Martin Luther King.

I grabbed a donut and a paper cup of coffee. Ted did the same and followed me into the auditorium where the debate had been held. Though the stage was dark I could see the outlines of the rostrums. The TV people had cleared all their equipment away.

We sat in theater chairs near the back.

'We won twice tonight,' Ted said.

I must have been thinking about those political ghosts. Something had distracted me, anyway. 'What?'

'I said we won twice tonight. First the debate and now the shooting. You think we aren't going to get a big sympathy vote?' The mannequin face gleamed with real pleasure.

'Yeah, we really "won" all right. Your wife could've been killed. I guess we have a different idea of "winning."'

'But she *wasn't* killed, was she? Don't get sanctimonious with me, Dev. Thank God she wasn't killed. But since she wasn't, let's try to find a bright side to this. We should get a bounce out of both the debate and some right-wing bastard trying to murder her. So, any guesses what that bounce'll be?'

He was hopeless. 'The two combined – maybe three or four points.'

'Are you serious? I'm thinking more like six or seven.'

'Probably not.'

'You know some people are going to think that Dorsey was behind this.'

'Some people think they've been abducted by aliens.'

'Don't kid yourself. The way he talked about all his "patriots" tonight. It's not a big leap to think that one of them might have been the shooter.'

'But there was nothing in it for Dorsey. He'd caught up with us. He might even have been ahead until tonight. We're the ones who'll now get the sympathy vote.'

'Maybe, but that still doesn't rule out somebody in Dorsey's camp—'

Abby said, 'Mind if I join you?'

She sat in the row in front of us.

'What happens now, Dev?' Ted said.

'We start planning for the news deluge. Ted, you can be our spokesman.'

'Are you kidding?'

'No. Jess needs to rest and you're her husband. You'll talk about the gun culture, how lucky Jess was and how we now have to pass serious legislation. And, of course, hit all the points we make every day. You're good on television.'

'I appreciate your faith in me, Dev. I really do. This is an important venue.' Then, 'I can't wait to see that first poll.'

'I'm more interested in the major poll three days from now. Once things have had a chance to shake loose for a little while.'

'Me, too,' Abby said. 'These things evaporate pretty quickly.'

'Somebody trying to kill a congresswoman?'

'Well, I guess you've got a point, Ted,' she said. 'This probably isn't going to go away anytime soon.'

'By God, Abby finally agrees with me about something.'

'Ted, I agree with you all the time. You always forget that because once in a while I *dis*agree with you.'

'Am I really that vain, Abby?'

Fortunately, Abby didn't have to answer because a man I didn't recognize came to the left door of the auditorium and said, 'The policeman out front said he's just been told that they think they have the shooter in custody!'

EIGHT

There are places lonelier than hotel rooms, but few of them are above ground.

At midnight I sat at a table in my nicely furnished small room in the Royale Hotel with my Mac open and CNN on the TV. All the cable channels except the right-wing ones were orgasming over the attempted assassination of Congresswoman Jessica Bradshaw.

As with most serious events, the first news had proved to be wrong. The police hadn't taken anybody into custody; they had questioned three 'persons of interest' which translated into three local men who had made notably ugly and violent remarks about Jess. Two had been turned in by acquaintances, and one by a family member, which was an interesting story by itself. For all the noise hate radio made, the majority of people did not want to see their elected officials threatened, let alone killed.

I'd called Chicago two hours ago and given one of my staffers there the job of answering the phones and redirecting any serious media calls we got to my cell phone here. So far I'd talked to two networks, including the news director of one of them. He'd made the best offer: seven minutes on the news. He was also planning a special called 'The Hate Merchants' and would give Jess seven more minutes on that. That would be on Friday night, a lame night for TV, but given the blanket coverage the shooting was getting it might pick up a much bigger audience than the night usually got. In the meantime, we had Ted on the most highly rated morning show.

So far I'd seen Trent Dorsey's hilarious response four times on CNN. He was sitting at a desk somewhere with shelves of fake books behind him and the edges of a giant green plastic plant showing on screen right. Local TV.

'I don't even care about winning anymore. I just want to know that Jessica Bradshaw is all right and I want to know that the person responsible is behind bars. The congresswoman and I have our disagreements but not about how our democratic election process should proceed. That's why I've been promoting the idea that our president should start using his office to promote fellowship, not the kind of ideas that divide this country. He knows where to find the answers to all our ills.'

Here he held up a small Bible, as if he was going to hawk it along with a bunch of other goodies 'if you ordered right now.'

'This is where the answers are, Mr President. Right here. And Jessica, my friend, if you're watching I hope you find a little time for the Good Book tonight. Nothing will give you more comfort, as my wife and our three kids learn every day of our lives. God bless America, folks. God bless America.'

The closest vomitorium was four cold blocks away. I was too tired to walk to it.

My daughter called a few minutes later, upset about the shooting and worried about me. She then told me about the granddaughter of mine she was carrying in her sixth month. Sarah's voice always redeemed me. Even though I was talking to a woman, I was also talking to a girl whose mere name inspired all the sentimental moments of her early life. How her face glowed in the candlelight from her fourth birthday cake; how she'd had a two-line part in the second-grade play; how beautiful she'd looked in that new dress the night of her ninth-grade dance. And then, the remorse for never being there enough for her. How she said she'd forgiven me for that once she'd grown up. But I couldn't forgive myself. That would be too easy.

Her 'I sure love you, Daddy' was the security blanket I needed tonight.

Then I felt the fatigue. I sat there watching the TV screen, slumped in the chair. Later I dragged myself to the john and then to bed.

I dreamed of the Zapruder tape. Jack and Jackie in the convertible. Jack lurching forward suddenly. Jackie leaning into him. The convertible speeding off. And then unreasonably, insanely, Jess was in a similar convertible, her head splintering in three pieces as it would in a horror movie. Ted was her Jackie. Leaning into her—

The phone woke me.

'I'm sorry to disturb you, Mr Conrad. I'm calling from the desk downstairs. There's a woman here who'd like to see you. I'm actually calling from the office instead of the desk so I can tell you about her.'

I struggled to wake up, to focus.

'She's very . . . disturbed. Scared, I'd say.'

'And she wants to talk to me?'

'She says it's urgent.'

The shooting. A woman with information.

'Is the bar still open?'

'For the next twenty minutes.'

'Ask her if she'll wait for me there. I'll be down right away.'

'All right.'

I moved in a daze. Cold water on my face. A hairbrush. Stepped quickly into my trousers and almost fell over. Loafers. Screw the socks. My very wrinkled shirt.

The elevator. Way too slow.

Crossed the empty lobby to the desk.

The tall young man in the hotel's red blazer was watching me from behind the counter. 'I hate to say this, Mr Conrad, but she left.'

'She didn't go into the bar?'

'No.' The long, thin face was way too somber for someone in his early twenties. 'I got another call here – a very angry guest – and while I was on it she got a call on her cell. I could hear her arguing with somebody and then she sounded kind of . . . pleading, I guess you'd say. I don't know what the other person said but it obviously got to her. She just turned around, started walking very quickly to the front doors and disappeared.'

'She ever give you her name?'

'No. I'm sorry.'

'What'd she look like?'

'Young – around thirty, I'd say. Pretty. Dark raincoat.'

I walked outside. There was a cab stand half a block west. A lone cab sat there. I went up to the driver's door and knocked on the window. The wind was making a metal racket with anything loose. Scents of cold and impending rain made the now moonless night bleaker. The blinking red light at the intersection signaled a disturbing urgency.

When the cab driver's window came down a heavy cloud of smoke escaped, along with the sounds of an excited radio minister. A fake gold cross hung from his rearview mirror.

'Yeah?' He was an older white guy in a heavy blue sweater.

'Did a cab just leave here?'

His whole wary life was in his green eyes. He had survived by being careful about what he said, and by judging people quickly. I was not likely to find favor with him.

'Why would you want to know?'

'I lost my woman.' I smiled. 'Had a little argument and she ran off.'

'She your wife?' The minister was in full rant now. The driver would want me to be a good, faithful husband.

'Of course.' I shrugged. 'She wants a new kitchen and I said we can't afford it. We really got into it. I overdid it. She ran out.'

His turn to shrug. 'Seen a lady get into Betty's cab a few minutes ago. Pretty good guess she was takin' your old lady home, don't you think?'

'Betty be back here tonight?'

'Maybe, maybe not.'

And with that his window went up.

Upstairs in my room, I called the cab company and identified myself as Jess's campaign manager. With the shooting my position gave me real gravitas.

'You have a driver named Betty.'

'Betty Cairns, yeah.'

'She picked up a woman at the Royale Hotel maybe ten minutes ago. Fifteen at the most. I'd really like to know where she took her.'

'Is this some kind of official business?'

'It could be. I really can't say anymore.'

'Official, huh?' He sounded amused. 'Gimme your phone number and I'll have her call you.'

There'd be no sleep for me until I heard from Betty. I read all the national coverage I could find on the shooting. Even the conservative papers were charitable to Jess's liberal voting record. The right-wing blogs were another matter. A few of them came close to suggesting that maybe this wouldn't be such a bad way to get rid of a Commie. My side had said similar nasty things when a right-wing senator had been seriously wounded in a hunting accident.

The local police chief's name was Aaron Showalter. He'd given Channel 6 a three-minute interview that I'd missed. I was watching the rerun now. He stood in front of the police department. Next to him was a very attractive, small and dark-haired woman he introduced as Detective Karen Foster. She was apparently a prop. She was not asked a single question.

Showalter looked and sounded ex-military in the interview. He had a thickset body and deliberate way of speaking and moving. He seemed smart and cautious. He didn't say much in the three minutes but managed to impress me as being harsh and wily.

The white Stetson almost ruined the hard-ass effect he wanted. If you live in Texas, Wyoming or South Dakota, the Stetson is fine, legit. If you live in a crooked river city in Illinois, you're just playing cowpoke. That he wore it while he was inside was even more of a joke. But even with the Stetson, I knew he would be dangerous.

If I remembered my law correctly, Showalter would now be part of an inter-agency task force (local agencies, state agencies and the regional FBI office) that would be assembled quickly to investigate the shooting. Most likely the state would assign security to travel with Jessica and protect her twenty-four-seven, which would be divided into three teams.

Betty called twenty minutes after I talked to the cab company. She had a soft, intelligent voice. 'I got a message to call you.'

'Thanks very much for getting back to me so soon.'

'They tell me you work for Congresswoman Bradshaw.'

'That's right.'

'Back when she was on the city council here – that was quite a while ago – she really fought to get us cabbies better wages. I've always appreciated that. I'm just glad she's all right. You wanted to know about my fare from the hotel, right?'

'Yes.'

'I took her over to the Skylight tavern. You know where that is?'

'I'm afraid I don't.'

'Over by the old baseball stadium. It was a decent place till they built the new stadium but now it's kind of a pit. That's where I took her.'

'Did she say anything while she was in your cab?'

'She cried a little on and off. Not much. She kept punching in numbers on her cell phone but it must've been busy or something because she'd cuss every time she tried.'

'Did you see anybody outside the place waiting for her?'

'No. And she couldn't have stayed too long. Earl, the guy who owns the place, was already cutting the lights. I wish there was more I could tell you.'

'This is very helpful, Betty. Very helpful.'

She yawned. 'Sorry. It's time for me to pack it in. I've got a husband at home who always makes breakfast for me no matter what time I roll in. That and bed sound pretty darned good right now.'

'Thanks, Betty. I really appreciate the call.'

Finding sleep again was difficult. It teased me. I almost dozed off several times, but not quite. It was the thought of how easy it would be if the woman who'd wanted to talk to me at the Royale could lead us directly to the shooter. But was anything ever that easy? So preposterously easy?

NINE

Jess and Ted lived in a Tudor-style house that could easily be classified as a mansion. At six-fifteen in the morning two massive TV trucks and at least half-a-dozen cars were parked in front of the wide steps leading up to the house itself. Dew made the vast slope of grass sparkle. A beautiful golden retriever – Churchill, as Jess had named him – roamed the front of the place.

Ted had called me at five-thirty. I'd asked him why he wanted me there. 'You know how these cocksuckers are.'

'Which cocksuckers are we talking about?'

'The network news cocksuckers. They know everything and you're just some dumb hick. But you know how to handle them. I'd like you to keep them from pushing me around.'

'I'm not sure I can do that. They don't have any more respect for me than for you.'

'I have this black turtleneck sweater. I don't know if you've noticed but I've developed this tiny gut. The sweater hides it. But the segment producer says that black is wrong. I had to show him four sweaters. He thinks the light blue one is best. First of all, it's fucking fall, all right? Who wears light blue anything in the fall? And second, it emphasizes my little gut. You see what I'm talking about?'

'Yeah, I see.' I wished I could roll my eyes the way Abby could. Man, when *she* rolled her eyes you were not only judged guilty, you were sentenced to death.

Five-thirty in the morning and he was laying fashion quibbles on me.

'No offense, Dev, but maybe you should've gone with another network.'

'Uh-huh. Well, listen, I need to shower and grab some breakfast, then I'll be at your place.'

'I really appreciate this, Dev. We've had our differences but that's going to change. From now on I'll listen to you. You're the expert.'

A magnanimous man is mighty Caesar.

I was about to ask how Jess was when he said, 'Get out here as fast as you can,' and hung up.

Despite the rush from His Majesty, I took three minutes to call Showalter's office. He wasn't there. I told the officer who answered about the young woman who'd called me, and how I wondered if this was worth pursuing.

Now, seated at the top of the stairs, Katherine gave me one of her wan little waves and followed it with one of her pale little smiles. She wore a simple white T-shirt, jeans, white socks and running shoes. She was colt spindly and all the more endearing for it.

'It's real stressful in there. I don't think I could work in TV. I had to come out here.' Her rich blonde hair gleamed in the early sunlight.

'That's because they've got to do a live cut-in. You don't get any chance to do it again. There's a lot of pressure.'

'My dad always says he's good under pressure. Mom always disagrees and I think she's right. This guy is kind of pushy. But my dad lost his temper right away.' She was watching Churchill bounce elegantly around the yard. 'It's probably nice being a dog. I know that sounds stupid but I think about it sometimes.'

'Doesn't sound stupid to me. I've thought of that all my life. Being a dog. A cat. A horse. Different kinds of animals.'

'I love cats. I bet being a cat would be nice sometimes.'

'In the first office I had we found a stray kitten. She'd lie next to my computer when I was working. And at night, when nobody else was around, I'd talk to her.'

'You were afraid what people would think if you talked to her during the day, huh?'

'Yeah, you know: "There goes the boss again, talking to his cat all day long."'

Hers was the fetching smile of her mom's.

'I wish I'd had you around when I was so sick, Dev. Thank God I had Uncle Joel and Nan. They always came to see me. I even started going to Mass and I'm not even Catholic.'

'The Vatican will be glad to hear that.'

She poked my arm with a tiny finger and laughed. It was time to stand up and go inside.

'I just feel so sorry for my dad. All the pressure he's under and he's not holding up very well.'

'I'd better get in there, honey. I'll see you in a little while.'

'Maybe you'll want to get out of there as quickly as I did.'

'I guess we're about to find out.'

A state trooper stood next to the massive medieval-style front door. He nodded his campaign hat at me. 'Need to see some ID, sir. You know the Bradshaw girl so I'm sure you're all right, but I'd still better check your ID.'

As far back as I could remember there were front and back doors, and sliding doors in the living room that opened onto an enormous patio for parties. There would be a trooper twenty-four-seven at each of these.

My ID checked, I walked inside.

Some people with mansions hang framed reproductions of the masters in their hallways. Not the Bradshaws. They went for posters from their campaigns. Here was Jess in the center of a flower burst of tiny black children – she might have been a missionary in Africa; here was Jess looking lovely and stern as she visited a bandaged soldier in a hospital; here were Jess and Ted addressing a grade-school class. There were numerous others. The sole non-campaign photo was of Jess and Ted standing in front of a rear extension to their mansion, taken a year or so ago. In the background was Joel with a heavyset and heavily bearded worker. And next to Joel, almost clinging to him was an anxious Katherine.

There was so much noise coming from one of the rooms down the hall, I imagined that the normally staid house must have felt violated. It was rough, almost angry language, the sound of a substantial crew racing to get everything in place before the unforgiving deadline.

Jess's assistant's name was Nan Winters. A slender, efficient, fiftyish woman dressed in a tan blouse and brown slacks, she came abruptly out of the den where the interview was being held. She waved. We were on friendly terms.

'Ted isn't used to being pushed around like this. I almost feel sorry for him.' The playful tone revealed the secret we shared. She loved Jess but thought Ted was a bit of a, to use her word, 'pill.' Technically she was Jess's assistant, but she never protested when her legendary cooking skills were put to use.

'I can't stand being in there. Everybody's so uptight.'

'That's what Katherine was telling me.'

'She is such a sweetie. I really got to know her in the hospital. Jess and Ted were so busy they didn't get much of a chance to visit her, so they asked me to sort of substitute. I got so I couldn't wait to get to the hospital. It was so nice to see her get better. I raised two boys but now I have the daughter I always wanted.'

I pointed to the den. 'I'd better go.'

'Good luck.'

The director was one of those guys who wore a sweater flung over his shoulders and tied at the front. He was also one of those guys who talked with his hands on his hips. He was small and masculine in an adversarial way. The den was a jungle of cables, lights, techs and miniature boxlike pieces of equipment planted everywhere like land mines.

'Greg, did you notice how sweaty his face is?' he said, irritated. 'Please pay some fricking attention, will you?' He was a man in bad need of a drink or a Xanax or some sex. Any one of them would do the trick.

Greg, a heavy man dressed in a khaki shirt and chinos, sighed and shook his head.

He stepped across all the cables and around all the equipment to reach Ted, who sat in a wing chair in front of the massive stone fireplace. I would not have put him there. This advertised the wealth of the Bradshaws, something we tried to keep secret as much as possible.

Greg was already tamping the sweat with a cloth. Seeing me, Ted shoved Greg's hand away and said, 'Thank God you're here, Dev. Will you please tell Roger that I look better in a sweater than in this piece-of-shit blue shirt? He invited himself into my closet to find it.'

'Roger Hallahan.' He jabbed his hand at me then proceeded to play bone-crusher. 'So you're Conrad. The way Mr Bradshaw talked about you I expected you to punch me out the second you saw me.'

'What's the problem?'

'The problem,' Ted said, 'is that "Roger" here won't let me wear my black sweater, remember? And he's practically written out a script.' He gave 'Roger' the kind of emphasis normally reserved for something brown the dog left on the floor.

Now it was Roger's turn to sigh. He had miniature Irish features that were somehow handsome all together on a large head. 'You're a pro, or that's what they tell me. Mr Bradshaw is worried about his alleged belly showing. Black is wrong in a dark room like this, and the shirt he's wearing sort of blouses at the belly so there's not even a hint of it – not that I can see it in the first place. We never see below his sternum.'

'See how he makes me sound, Dev? My wife was almost assassinated last night and he makes me sound like some vain pussy who doesn't give a shit about it. I want to look good for *her* sake. I'm representing *her*. He has me looking like some guy who sits around in a shirt all day.'

'Maybe you haven't noticed, Mr Bradshaw, but shirts are "in" now. A lot of very powerful men wear shirts to the office and shirts to parties.'

Finally, it was my turn to sigh. 'Roger, how long before the network picks us up?'

He glanced at the Rolex on his wrist. He clicked the stopwatch.

I could tell because the ticking was loud in the momentary silence. 'Seven minutes and thirty-one seconds.'

'How about you give me one minute and thirty seconds in the hall?'

He was as eager to get out of the den as he would have been to get off the *Titanic*.

'Fine.'

I didn't much like him but I felt professionally sorry for him. All he wanted to do was make Ted look and sound as good as possible. But, as usual, Ted was determined to get his own way.

In the hall, Roger said, 'You going to give me shit, too?'

TEN

'**N**o. I agree with you. But you'll get a better interview if you let him wear the black turtleneck.'

'A turtleneck's wrong for this and so is black.'

'You know that and I know that, but he's used to getting his way.'

'How the hell do you put up with it?'

'I go along till I have to tell him I'll quit if he gets his way.'

'There's no time for that with this little gig.'

'No.'

'Does he give a shit about his wife? I really get the impression he couldn't care less.'

'I actually think he does.'

'Well, he's got a strange way of showing it.' For the first time the small, beleaguered man smiled. 'Let's go get the fucking sweater.'

Back in the den, I went over to Ted and said, 'Is the sweater still upstairs?'

'You did it, didn't you? I *knew* you could do it.' Then, 'Hey, Greg, how about bringing that sweater over here?' It was as if a six-year-old had just been handed a three-scoop ice-cream cone on a hot summer day.

As soon as the network morning show began, three different monitors telecast the proceedings. There was three minutes of news leading with Jess's story, then back to the chirpy personas of the hosts, and then the chief host wiped both the silly grin and lusty gaze away (the substitute hostess was a true babe) and said, 'In addition to mass murders and terrorism, our country now has to turn a serious eye to the possibility of political assassination. Last night in Danton, Illinois, an unknown shooter attempted to assassinate Congresswoman Jessica Bradshaw as she left the building where she'd just debated her opponent on television. Fortunately the three shots did not find their target, but they certainly left the congresswoman and her staff, including her husband, concerned for her safety. As they did, I might say, the entire country.

'Here now from the Bradshaw home is Ted Bradshaw, a man well known in Washington for his political skills, where he works closely with his wife in fighting for the legislation they believe in. He is considered a role model for the modern Congressional spouse. Good morning, Mr Bradshaw.'

'Ted is fine.'

In the vast universe all eyes were focused on him and the black turtleneck that – surprise! – only seemed to enhance the bulk of his little tummy. Even through the screen you could feel the emanations of ecstasy that must be putting him in heart-attack range.

I'm on network TV!

Fortunately, he wasn't bad at fake solemnity. And mixed in with the fake solemnity there was no doubt some honest solemnity. He loved Jess; he feared for her. And always pressing on the edges of his consciousness were thoughts of her someday Senate run. Imagine the kind of respect he'd get at the D.C. parties when he was the hubby-wubby of a senator.

The interview was pretty good. Host and guest were both practiced at said fake solemnity. They discussed how the local police had joined the state police and an FBI agent to search for the shooter, and said that the congresswoman was resting and was under twenty-four-seven state trooper protection.

Then the questions: what is this country coming to? Wasn't it wonderful that House members from both sides were overwhelming her with praise? Was the murder attempt the inevitable result of our gun culture? When will the congresswoman be back on the campaign trail? What is this country coming to?

Then it was over.

Roger Hallahan stepped in and said, 'You did a good job, Mr Bradshaw. Thank you. And give my best to your wife.'

'Change your mind about the turtleneck yet?'

I felt sorry for Hallahan. Ted not only had to be right, he had to punish you for not having agreed with him.

'Yeah,' Hallahan said, a familiar weariness in his voice, the weariness that all operatives feel working with the Ted Bradshaws of politics. 'Yeah, you looked great.'

I left the den abruptly. It was too early in the day for the ass-kissing Ted would require. I have a rule about that. No ass-kissing before ten-thirty. Before then it causes acute acid reflux.

In the hall, I found Nan. 'You happen to know where Jess is?'

'I just fixed her two eggs, toast and coffee, and she's sitting alone on the patio. I'm sure she'd love some company.'

She was wearing sandals, jeans and a crisp, white short-sleeved blouse. The breakfast Nan had prepared for her was down to a single half-slice of toast. A delicately sculpted silver coffeepot was next to her on the table. The beautiful blue of cigarette smoke coiled up from a tiny faux Mandarin-style ashtray. There was a symphony of morning birds and the cool, thin shadows of early morning. It was so idyllic, it was easy to forget that the woman sitting here had almost been shot to death less than twelve hours ago.

'Don't ask me how I'm feeling.'

'All right.'

'But please sit down.'

'Thank you.'

'Coffee?'

'Please.'

'You've noticed the cigarette?'

'I've noticed the cigarette. Hard to miss.'

'First one in eighteen years. Since I was in college.'

'I'd say it's well deserved.'

'How do you like the coffee? Nan made it.'

'It's very good.'

There was an atonal quality to her voice. Almost as if she'd been drugged. And maybe she had.

'How did Ted do?'

'You didn't watch?'

'I was too afraid for him. It's not easy for him, living in my shadow.'

'He did very well.'

'You don't like him, do you?'

What the hell. 'I don't hate him.'

The laugh was the first sign of her usual self. 'Was that supposed to be diplomatic?'

'Sort of.'

She took a deep drag of her cigarette. The pack had been depleted by several smokes. 'I wish Ted had a little of you in him and I wish you had a little of Ted in you. He can be a child a lot of the time, but there's a sweetness to him.'

'Tell me where they sell it and I'll buy some.'

She tilted her head back and closed her eyes. 'But you're a lot more reassuring than he is. Tell me not to be afraid. I'm feeling a little bit paralyzed right now.'

'When I get the chance to speak to the chief of police—'

'You'll get that chance in a few minutes. He's on his way out here to talk to me.'

'Good.'

'So what about me being so afraid?' She watched me again.

'I'm glad you're afraid. That means you're taking this seriously. And that means you'll do everything the police and the state troopers tell you to do. I was afraid you'd insist on going right back to walking rope lines again. Shaking hands. Meet and greets.'

'They tell me I'm pretty good at it.'

'You're excellent at it. But we're going to change your schedule so you're in situations where security can really protect you. Every appearance will be indoors until further notice. I can guarantee you they'll insist on that.'

I saw the chief of police through the glass doors. He was even more military in person than he had been on the screen. He moved in quick, certain steps.

'Sorry I'm late, Congresswoman. I'm sorry I have to put you through this.'

'Chief Showalter, this is my friend and campaign manager, Dev Conrad.'

He had a hard, calloused hand. This morning he wore a white button-down shirt under a black leather jacket of the fashionable kind. Gray slacks and black loafers completed the attire. And being a cowpoke, he still wore that damned white Stetson. He at least took it off now in deference to the lady. Cowpokes are nothing if not polite.

He then introduced the appealing Detective Karen Foster, who'd stood silently by him in his TV interview. Today the suit was an autumn brownish-red. She shook hands with Jess and then with me. I liked to think that she held my hand a little longer than necessary because she thought I was downright irresistible.

Showalter did the talking for the next five minutes. He advanced a few theories which didn't sound plausible, said that he had even more officers going over the area where the shooter had stood now that it was daylight, and assured Jess that the shooter would be identified and apprehended. He wisely didn't put forth a time when this miracle of detection was going to take place.

Meanwhile, Detective Foster kept watching me. Not just looking at me, *watching* me, as if she thought I was going to do something suspicious. At least I wasn't foolish enough to interpret the scrutiny of those dark eyes as reflecting any romantic or sexual interest in me. But then she smiled at me. She hadn't spoken a single word since talking briefly with Jess. Then the watching. And now the smile. Neither Jess nor Showalter seemed to notice it. I luxuriated in it.

Showalter was still the man in charge. He'd started lifting his Stetson up and then setting it back down. Maybe he was lonely without it.

'When I talked to the congresswoman earlier, Mr Conrad, I told her about the information you left with my office this morning. We're following it up right now.'

'I hope I'm not wasting your time.'

'I Googled you. Since you were an army investigator you should know how these things go. This could be nothing but I need to follow it down. I had an officer at the Skylight at seven o'clock this morning. The day man wasn't much help. He gave my man the home phone number of the night bartender but says the night man shacks up with different female customers, so he wasn't sure he could contact him until he showed up for work.'

'That's almost funny,' Jess said.

'You should see the kind of women who hang out down there. My people have to go there six, seven times a week.'

'Just think if she actually knew something,' Jess said.

Nan walked on the patio bearing a second coffeepot that appeared to be identical to the one on the table.

'If you'll excuse me, Jess, Abby and I need to get working on your schedule for the next couple days,' I said. 'I'll call you as soon as we have something ready. And if you don't like it, obviously we'll change it.'

'You really need to leave?'

'I do. And the chief here will have plenty of questions to keep you busy.'

Then Ted was there. In his mind he was accepting a Daytime Emmy Award for Best Performance before Eight A.M.

Ted went immediately to Jess, kissed her on the cheek and sat down.

'Dev tells me you did very well with the interview, honey.'

'You didn't watch?'

The little boy again: his mom had missed the game where he'd hit his home run.

Showalter said, 'Well, we've got a few more things besides TV to talk about here. I'd like you to stay, Mr Bradshaw. I'll have several questions for you, too.'

'Really? Now?'

This actually sounded like the kind of work that just might get in the way of calling a few thousand friends. He'd want to know if they'd seen the interview and, if they had, just how fabulously fabulous they thought he'd done.

'Well, I need to go and get to work,' I said.

Showalter did not look amused.

But Detective Foster did. This time her smile made me want to propose living together or maybe even tying the knot. Something was going on here. Despite the superficial flattery of her seeming interest, she struck me as far too intelligent for teases. Those eyes were as shrewd and knowing as they were lovely. She wanted something from me.

I was heading for the door when I heard, from the living room, the music of Katherine's laughter. After all she survived and all she might still face, her laugh, as melodramatic as this might sound, was an affirmation of life from someone who appreciated it, unlike a lot of us who bitch and kvetch about it with oblivious disdain.

I should have guessed she was with Joel. They sat on the loveseat near the grand piano and, as always, she seemed even more radiant in his presence, a radiance I never saw when she was with her parents. Joel paid attention to her – something I suspected she didn't get much of from either Jess or Ted. They sat in the shimmering autumn sunlight, and fine figures they were.

'Both my boyfriends at the same time. Come and sit down with us, Dev.' Katherine smiled.

Joel had told me that Katherine always developed crushes on the older men who spent time with her.

'One of us'll get jealous in a minute,' I said to her as I sat in an armchair across from them.

'I wish I had a jealous boyfriend. I was going with this boy from Northwestern before I got sick. He still calls me sometimes but I think it's out of duty, which makes me feel sorry for him. He's a good guy. We weren't ever in love or anything serious. We'd just started dating before I got sick. But he still doesn't want me to feel deserted or anything.'

As she spoke I shifted my attention from Katherine to Joel. His blue eyes showed pain. She wasn't trying to be noble, she was just stating facts. She didn't even sound all that hurt about the guilty boy moving on. But Joel's gaze reflected the hurt he felt for her. No wonder she liked her Uncle Joel so much.

He changed the subject abruptly. 'I wish I'd seen you before you started talking to Showalter,' he said to me.

'I take it you don't like him.'

'Like doesn't matter. But trust does.'

'Why don't you trust him?'

'He's hunting buddies with Dorsey. And bowling buddies. And Friday night football buddies. They both were jocks in high school.'

'None of that sounds good.'

Nobody knew as much bad news as Joel Bradshaw. It wasn't that he enjoyed it, but he knew he needed to share it because that was the best way to address it.

'Dorsey's got this big anti-crime photo op coming up. The usual thing. Candidate in front and a wall of cops behind him.'

'Standard stuff.'

'It's scheduled for next Wednesday. A working day for some of the cops who'll be standing behind him. There's a town statute that forbids on-duty policemen to appear in any kind of promotional activity. It also forbids law enforcement officers to make any kind of political endorsements.'

'Thanks for letting me know. I'll talk to the mayor about it.'

'Won't do any good. Showalter has already convinced the mayor to waive the law in this case.'

'And the mayor agreed?'

'The mayor hates my mom, Dev. He's a good friend of Dorsey's, too.'

'Bowling does it every time,' I said. 'You get two guys to start bowling together and they'll be inseparable.'

Katherine's laugh was my reward.

Joel said, 'I'm just worried about how Showalter's going to handle it. He's really working as an agent for Dorsey. A dangerous one.' Then, 'But even he has limits to what he can do, I suppose.'

'Now you've really got me worried. You know the town a lot better than I do. I hope we don't have to get any kind of injunction for anything he tries because that might put us past the election before we could stop him.'

'I keep waiting to hear about those two guys who showed up with guns at the debate,' Katherine said. 'Aren't they likely suspects?'

'I'm assuming that Showalter is checking them out. If they are involved they're pretty dumb – showing up with guns and then trying to kill Jess a couple of hours later.'

'They're not exactly intellectuals, Dev.'

'I know. But still—'

'Maybe they left there and poured down some liquor and talked themselves into giving it a try.'

'That's possible. But they didn't really hassle the security people or the police. They got turned away and just got in their car and left.'

Nan strode into the room. 'Is anybody ready for a snack?'

'I wish I could, Nan. But I need to get going.'

'You always need to get going, Dev. One of these times you'll actually sit down and let me make you a good lunch.'

'I've had several dinners here before.'

'Catered. For special events I'm just the greeter. A chef comes in. He won't let me in the kitchen.'

'He's really a snob,' Katherine said. 'I don't like him. I don't even think his name is André Babineaux.'

'What do you think his name really is?' I asked as I started to leave.

'I don't know about the last name, but his first name is Bubba.'

'I like that,' Nan said. 'Bubba Babineaux.'

ELEVEN

A bby and I spent five straight hours working on a new schedule for Jess.

She knew all the local people and all the local venues so she'd make suggestions, and if we both agreed she'd place the calls. We wanted sites an assassin couldn't penetrate, knowing that no such site existed. Just because he'd used a powerful rifle last night didn't mean that he couldn't sneak in a handgun today. I called our final choices into Showalter's office and his administrative assistant said he'd call us back after he'd looked them over.

In the meantime, I had to check on the other races my office was running. We had new internals on all of them. The majority of them looked good; two were disasters. Pair two less-than-stellar candidates against several million in dark money and victory is going to be elusive.

The phone rang at the receptionist's desk and half a minute later Donna Watson buzzed and said it was for me. Abby waved goodbye and left.

As soon as I said hello, a woman's voice said, 'Thanks to you I have to hide out. You have the police looking for me.' The day bartender had called her. My mystery friend from last night.

'You need to talk to the police.'

'Well, I don't want to talk to them.'

'You may have information about the person who tried to kill Congresswoman Bradshaw last night.'

'He needs help. I want to help him. If the police get involved they like to shoot people.'

'Apparently so does he. Are we talking about your husband?'

But she said only what she wanted to say. 'His third tour in Afghanistan really changed him.'

'I'm sorry. If he needs help then I'll let the police chief know that and he can arrange to handle this without any threat of violence.'

'I'm not sure I believe that.'

'So what are you proposing to do?'

'I'd like you to talk to him.'

'Does he know about this call?'

'No. Before I tell him about it I want your word that you'll talk to him before you call the police.'

'I don't know if I can do that.'

'Why not?'

'Because I could be accused of harboring a felon.'

'He's my husband. And I know he's in some kind of trouble. I found six thousand dollars in cash in his underwear drawer. He was trying to hide it. He hires out as a landscaper to work on crews at not much more than minimum wage. I don't know where he'd get that kind of money.'

'So how do we resolve this?'

'I need you to be at a certain place tonight at ten o'clock and I need your solemn word you won't tell the police. I'll explain when I see you.'

If that was the only way I could move this along, fine. Showalter wouldn't like it, but if we could identify our man and then apprehend him, Showalter couldn't complain for too long.

'Where?'

'Do you know where the houseboats are tied up in Tomlin Park?'

'No.'

'Just ask somebody.'

'All right.'

'At the east end of the area there's a pavilion. At that time of night on a weeknight nobody'll be using it. My husband and I will be inside. Waiting for you.'

'I hate to say this, but your husband may have tried to kill the congresswoman last night. To me that makes him a dangerous man. I won't have any protection at all if he decides to shoot me.'

'I can't believe you think he could kill somebody. You don't even know him. For your information, he'll be unarmed. I'll make sure of it. I promise.'

He might be unarmed. But I wouldn't be.

'What if I tell him that I want to call the police on my cell phone and have them take him in for questioning?'

'He's pretty scared right now. I'll tell him that you'll bring that up.'

'So he's thought about what he did last night and he's scared?'

'We'll talk about it tonight. I'm at work right now and I need to go.'

I scribbled quick notes about the conversation. I wanted to remember everything. Her remark about her husband being scared had seemed odd to me at first. But as I sat there going back over everything she'd said I realized how natural it would be for him to be afraid now. The excitement would overcome fear – planning it, practicing it, doing it. But not only had he failed to even hurt her, now he had to face a couple of hard facts. The cops would be everywhere searching for him. Relentlessly. And when they found him he would be going to prison for life. I'd be scared, too – damned scared.

'So you'll be there.'

'I'll be there.'

'And you won't bring the police.'

'I won't bring the police. I won't contact them beforehand.'

'How about afterward?'

'You're not a defense lawyer, are you?'

For the first time, she laughed. 'I sound like one, don't I? But really – will you contact them afterward?'

'Depends on how things work out.'

A pause. 'I guess that's fair.'

'As fair as it's going to get.'

'We'll see you tonight, then.' And she hung up.

Suddenly even the two elections we were likely to lose didn't seem as depressing as they had earlier. I went to work redrafting Jess's last two commercials.

TWELVE

I was standing at the window watching dusk turn the sky and the world below into a dolefully beautiful evening. In Chicago I might be in a bar having drinks with a woman who interested

me, hoping that I interested her as well. The old Mick maudlin side
always wrenched me in its self-pitying grip at this time.

'Hello!'

Young voice, male. Cory Tucker, the volunteer driver.

'In here, Cory.'

'I'm sorry if I interrupted anything.'

'You didn't. I was just thinking a little about the commercials
we do next. What's up?'

'Just thought I'd stop in and see what was going on. I finished
up my school work and thought I'd stop by and see if anybody
needed me.'

He was modest, capable and nice-looking in an upwardly mobile
way. In his V-neck blue sweater with the button-down white shirt
and the tan-colored slacks, not to mention the blonde crew cut, he
could have been a college boy in one of those old MGM musicals
my mom always watched on TV. That was his appearance, anyway.
But his enthusiasm bothered me. He seemed too bright to think that
being an ass-kisser would get him anywhere. He was a volunteer.
Even if he got a raise he'd go from zero dollars an hour to zero
dollars an hour. Dorsey's wet dream – slave labor. Sometimes I
wondered if he was overcompensating. But then the question was
overcompensating for what?

'I'm going to have to rent a car.' I needed one for the drive to
the houseboats.

'Hey, I'm your driver, remember?'

'If you really want something to do, I'm sure they can find you
plenty of work at the campaign headquarters.'

'I was there earlier. Boy, the mood has really changed. Nobody's
uptight about the election anymore.'

'Really?'

'Yeah. They figure that we'll win for sure after . . . after what
happened last night.'

'That's not very smart. We have two weeks to go before the
election. Anything could happen.'

'That's what they're worried about now. Not getting out the vote
and stuff like that. They're worried about whether the congresswoman is going to be alive. A couple of the girls were crying when
I was talking to them about it. They're really scared.'

'Tell them she's under full twenty-four-seven protection.'

'They're wondering why she's going right back out tomorrow.'

I wondered if he'd come here as a kind of unofficial spokesperson for the volunteers at headquarters. Of course they'd be worried. Of course they'd be afraid that there might be a second attempt and that maybe the second attempt would be successful. And of course I should haul my ass down there and talk to them – something I should have done several hours ago.

'You know what, Cory?'

'What?'

'I could use a ride to headquarters.'

'They'll really appreciate it, Dev. They trust Abby and all but they see her every day. You're from out of town and you've been doing this most of your life. And you were an army investigator. I mentioned that several times to them. I'll mention it again when I tell them that you want to talk to them.'

I hadn't spent much time at campaign headquarters. This was a good excuse.

There were maybe twenty people at campaign headquarters. Most of them were working the phone banks.

I wasn't about to interrupt them with some lame pep talk.

The cliché is that elections are won or lost based on the battle your supporters put on. That's somewhat overstated but not by too much. The phone calls, the door-to-door, the rallies, the outreach to various groups . . . all are critical elements in any victory. Only since the Supreme Court claimed that corporations are people, too – just neighbors as nice as can be – did the value of the supporters diminish somewhat. When millions are poured into a Congressional battle like Jessica Bradshaw's, cash dominates everything else.

A woman named Jean Fellows had been a reporter before retiring. She was second in command here. She should have been first. All I'd heard about the number one, someone named Mary Schmidt, was that Jean had to follow her around and fix her mistakes. Schmidt's husband had contributed something like seventy thousand dollars to the coffers so his wife had her choice of positions.

Jean had a tiny office in the back of the place. As I walked back there I heard the eager, friendly voices of the phone workers. Once in a while they got attacked. They called somebody who believed that Jess had been born in Moscow and had won her Congressional

seat by using arcane black magic on the voters. The good phone
workers know to just excuse themselves and hang up when all this
starts. The bad ones stay on the line and fight. It's useless to try
and persuade the tinfoil hat brigade, but I have to admit – having
been a bad phone worker myself way back when I was in college
– it makes you feel one hell of a lot better than just hanging up.

Jean was just wrapping up a phone conversation reminding somebody in a terse, vaguely threatening voice that the two billboards
that had been promised had yet to appear over on Sixteenth and
Twenty-first avenues respectively and that certain people – namely
one Jean Fellows – would be mightily displeased if they did not
appear within the next six hours. She hung up, shaking her head.

Jean was given to jumpers and Navajo jewelry. She had a strong
handshake and a somewhat accusatory brown gaze, as if you were
going to sell her a car that would fall apart one week after she
signed the papers. She also had fluffy and elegant pure white hair.

'Slumming, huh, Dev?'

She'd visited our Chicago offices with Ted one time and we'd
taken to each other immediately.

'Yeah. I figured this'd be a good place to score some meth and
some hookers.'

'You joke, but we've had a few volunteers here over the three
campaigns that really worried me. There was a college senior who
was sleeping with a fifteen-year-old girl. He dumped her, of course,
and, of course, she went right to her parents – which she should've
done. Which *I* would've wanted *my* daughter to do – obviously I
would've preferred that she not start sleeping with the jerk in the
first place – but the parents decided against bringing charges because
of how it would affect their daughter. You think that wasn't terrifying? It could've cost us the election. That year we won by less
than two points.'

That was one campaign horror story I hadn't heard. Jean wasn't
exaggerating. The other side spread so many false rumors. Was Jess
gay? Was she into threesomes? Was she transgendered? The press
would do the bidding for the other side with unmatched zeal; it was
always s-e-x, wasn't it?

'So how's Jess doing?'

'As far as I know, pretty good.'

'Between us, I'd be afraid to be in public again.'

'She's got a lot of protection but I'm nervous for her sake, too.'

'I saw Ted on TV this morning. He did a good job. But he loves the spotlight a little too much for my taste.'

'Well, let's say he did a good job and leave it at that.'

'Someday we'll have a *real* discussion about Ted Bradshaw and I'm going to *force* you to tell me what you think of him.'

Her phone rang. She went into field commander mode again. Apparently there was a sector of the city that had not been visited by our volunteers. She was relaying her feelings about this in a voice that would have done George S. Patton proud. Whoever was on the other end of the phone was no doubt cowering and getting ready to beg for mercy.

After she hung up, she said, 'By the way, you hear what a caller said on Phil Michaels's show?'

Michaels was our local hate-radio guy.

'The caller said he hoped that next time there'd be a better shooter and Michaels said he'd be willing to pay for target practice at a firing range.'

'You're actually surprised? I'm not.'

'In my day if you said something like that two of J. Edgar Hoover's boys would pay you a visit.'

'That dates you right there.'

'What does?'

'J. Edgar Hoover. He was a long time ago.'

'Yes, he was, sonny boy.' Her harsh laugh was a salute to the institutions of tobacco and alcohol. 'But the stench lingers on.' Then, 'I suppose you want to bore our gang with a pep talk?'

I slid my arm around her and hugged her. 'I'm thinking you and I would make a perfect couple.'

THIRTEEN

The dark waters reflected the moonlight. The yellow security lights swayed in the wind. Only one of the houseboats showed any light in its windows. The expensive craft were at the west end of the dock. The ones nearest the asphalt I stood on were not only modest, a few of them were in shambles. Paint faded, windows patched with tape, not much bigger than a prison cell. I doubted that these ever left the dock. They'd work for beer parties just fine as people, drinks and drugs sprawled over the land, keeping the shabby houseboats nothing more than storage bins. The elites at the far end of the dock probably roared up here just to stand on the bow and piss. It was strange then that the pavilion would be at my end. It was behind me in the wooded area. I'd checked it out. It was empty.

A politician is shot at. A minimum-wage landscaper has six thousand dollars cash in his underwear drawer. A woman who claims to be his wife woos me out here . . .

My rental was the only car in sight. There was no traffic on the river road, either. The surrounding timbered hills made me uneasy. After last night I'd become aware of all the places a sniper could hide.

The temperature had to be below forty now. I wore the collar of my Burberry turned up. My Glock was in my right pocket.

I watched as every few minutes cars drove east on the narrow river road. There was a new housing development about two miles from here. I kept waiting for one of the cars to crank down a turn signal and pull in here. Then the woman and her husband would appear and explain everything. And after they explained, we could bring in the police and the matter would be resolved.

I walked around to keep warm. The long line of watercraft should have been the scene of women in bikinis, cookouts and little kids proving that they were in fact powered by batteries. And husbands and wives happy to be together again after the long hard week of scraping together a living in these brutal and unforgiving economic times.

The pep talk at campaign headquarters had gone well for the twelve minutes it took to deliver it. How confident I'd sounded; how downright paternal. When you mention that you're working with the FBI, the state police and a security task force, most people buy in. For all the time they're listening, anyway. But then you leave and they start thinking and talking – you know how these damned human beings are, thinking and talking all the time – and all of a sudden it's as if that fatherly gent hadn't spoken at all.

But now it was just the attack of the branch-rattling wintry wind . . .

The clattering old Ford pickup truck came along a few minutes later, spewing country-western music and angry shouts. Then an image: the young woman and her husband bitterly arguing over talking to me. Him growing more and more dangerous the closer they got to me.

But no.

In a furious clamor, human and mechanical, the red pickup passed on, disappearing around the curve about a block east of here.

A few minutes later, another car. A newer Ford. Slowing down. Turning in.

I felt the beams of the headlights as they detailed me. A perfect target for any enterprising shooter.

The Ford kept on coming toward me. Then stopped jerkily. A white-haired man's head appeared through the open window. 'Could you help me?'

The voice was old and urgent.

Fingers around the Glock – who knew what the hell this was all about? – I made my way to the car. Seen up close, he looked very old indeed.

'The wife got me this GSP thing' – he meant GPS – 'but I forgot how to use it. I was just drivin' to the convenience store'n I got lost. I guess I should turn around, huh?'

'You want to go back to town?'

'Yeah. Then I want to get home.'

'Then you turn right around and head back on the river road. Town's just a couple miles away.'

The brown eyes were as worn as the lined face and the trembling voice.

I checked my watch again. I had been here just short of thirty-five minutes. And for no discernible reason.

'Tell you what. Let me get in my own car, then you can follow me into town.'

'That'd be real nice of you. This GSP thing ain't worth a damn.'

All the way back to the hotel I sulked and brooded. Maybe I was playing a game with a woman who didn't know a damned thing about the shooting. Hell, maybe Dorsey's people had put her on me just to run me around in circles.

Later, I ended up in the hotel bar talking to a woman who was at least as lonely as I was. She showed me a variety of grandkid photos – she looked to be a very young forty – and talked about all the night-school classes she'd been taking since her husband had left her for the younger woman he'd met at the gym. She was here visiting her sister and would be heading back to Grand Rapids tomorrow. Then she got a tad alcohol-sad and started dabbing her eyes, not only with her drink napkin but also with mine. And then, like quick cuts in a movie we were in the elevator, then in her room, and then in bed. It was comfort sex for both of us – nothing wrong with that at all.

FOURTEEN

The activities of the next day reminded me of my army days. Complicated maneuvers.

The task force responsible for Jess's protection had approved of the schedule we'd emailed them and then had responded accordingly by Google mapping every place we planned to go. The appropriate number of local and state police would be dispatched. Extra officers would be needed to control the swollen number of reporters. The three most desirable hotels were completely sold out. Jess was a national celebrity; the best kind, the kind you felt sorry for. Feared for.

Jess worked her way through the approved schedule. All photo ops – a retirement home, a new mattress factory Jess had wrangled massive tax cuts for, a farm family that would have been too sweet even for a Norman Rockwell painting. Jess had had no choice but to vote for the farm bill, a payoff to corporate agriculture that would make any sane person sick to his or her stomach. In addition to being thieves, they were also poisoning the worldwide food supply with pesticides and genetically modified organisms. But we'd voted for it, hadn't we? This was an election year and this was an agricultural state. We liked to think of ourselves as decent people; we also liked to think of ourselves as having a seat in the next Congress.

The press loved the drama. The TV people especially enjoyed asking average citizens about the shooting. One woman even teared

up talking about how afraid she was for poor Congresswoman
Bradshaw. Tears are the TV equivalent of orgasm.

Jess found the number of protectors excessive. Instead of
comforting her they reminded her of her vulnerability. It was easy
to imagine last night's gunshots playing over and over in her head.

Despite her annoyance and fears she was just about perfect in
the Q&As and was especially touching in a conversation with an
elderly couple in assisted living. The press loved it.

By early afternoon the appearances were over. Cory drove us
back to Jess's house. Jess wasn't the gloating sort, but I could tell
by the occasional playful smile that she was pleased with herself.
It didn't hurt that Cory reminded her every few minutes how well
she'd done.

A black Mercury sedan that could only be an unmarked police
car sat in front of the house. I was not only curious but for some
reason uneasy about this. I assumed that the Mercury was the property of Chief Showalter.

Once inside, Jess excused herself and said she was headed upstairs
to lie down. She didn't seem interested in the presence of the chief.

'Anything for me to do?' Cory asked.

'Go in the kitchen and get yourself a snack if you're hungry.'

'I could use a Pepsi.'

'There you go.'

'Just help myself?'

'Don't worry about that pit bull guarding the refrigerator. He
only attacks Dorsey supporters.'

He laughed and headed down the west hall.

Nan emerged from the living room. Worry crabbed her pleasant
face. 'Chief Showalter and Ted have been in the den for twenty
minutes or so. I heard Ted shout about ten minutes ago. I get the
feeling something's going on.'

'Maybe I'd better get in there.'

'Just knock.'

Which I did.

Showalter's voice invited me in. He was in charge. My anxiety
about him being here was proving to be correct.

The den was of Hollywood design. Massive built-in bookcases,
massive stone fireplace, massive Persian rugs over hardwood floors,
a desk you could perform surgery on and genuinely mullioned

windows. The dark leather furnishings would have made a British lord proud.

The ambience of the room was spoiled by the two men sitting in it.

'I'm glad you're here, Dev,' Ted said. 'I was about to say a couple of things to our esteemed chief of police.'

'I'm doing my job, Mr Bradshaw. Nothing more. I'm not accusing anybody of anything.' To me, Showalter said, 'We had a meeting at the station this morning. The whole crew, including Forensics, and a few questions came up. Mr Bradshaw is jumping to conclusions.'

'The hell I am. You're the one who's jumping to conclusions. You come in here with some bullshit about maybe the whole thing was faked—'

'Wait a minute. What the hell's that supposed to mean?'

'See, Dev, you're reacting the same way I did. It's total bullshit.'

There were two chairs in front of the aircraft-carrier-sized desk. Ted, being the commander, sat behind the desk; Showalter and I sat in front of it.

I said to the chief, 'I don't like the sound of that at all.'

'I don't blame you. I wouldn't like the sound of that, either. But that isn't what I said.'

'Go ahead and tell Dev what you told me. See how *he* reacts.'

Showalter's large head pivoted toward me. He angled himself in the chair so he faced me. 'I'll be happy to tell you what I told Mr Bradshaw. Hopefully, you'll appreciate the fact that I'm just doing my job of investigating. You were an investigator. You know you have to eliminate all the possibilities if you want to do an honest job.'

But Ted's charge that Showalter had said or implied that somehow the assassination was 'fake' had startled me. What the hell could Showalter be talking about?

'We looked at where the shooter was firing from. The trajectory. Then we studied where the bullets hit the building behind Congresswoman Bradshaw. They all hit well above her head.'

'So he was a lousy shot. I don't know why that's so important.' Ted's anger had now been replaced by whining.

'Do you see what I'm talking about, Mr Conrad?'

I shrugged. 'Either he was a total amateur or he panicked.'

'We're not ruling either of those possibilities out.' He tried to enlist my support again. 'I think you'll agree, Mr Conrad, that I'm just trying to do my job.'

'I can see that, Chief Showalter.'

'You're siding with him, Dev? Great. You're on *my* payroll, remember?'

'This is all speculation, Ted. The shots went wild. My personal feeling is that the shooter panicked. He wanted to kill Jess but he got scared.'

Showalter kept his face cop-blank as I spoke. Not even his eyes revealed any opinion.

'There. There's your answer. What Dev said. The bastard got scared at the last minute and his shots went wild. We're just lucky it happened that way or my poor wife would be dead.'

Showalter spoke quietly. 'Mr Bradshaw, you called me last night just before midnight. My wife and I happened to be sleeping. Our oldest daughter has strep and Becca was worn out. But I took your call and we talked for what, nearly twenty minutes? You said you wanted to be in the loop. You must have used that expression ten times. So I thought that as a courtesy I'd drive out here and let you know what we were thinking. All the scenarios we've considered so far,' he nodded to me, 'including what Mr Conrad said – that our shooter got scared and his shots went wild. We're obviously dealing with a disturbed personality here so who the hell knows what he was thinking. All we know is that he's dangerous and that we need to find him ASAP because we can't be sure he won't try it again. Which is why we've got the congresswoman protected seven ways from sundown.'

A couple of things were going on here. Number one was that Ted was getting the kind of treatment police officers reserve for the wealthy. If Ted had been middle class or, God forbid, working class or poor, Showalter would have said what was really on his mind. And he would have said it bluntly. As an accusation.

Number two was that Ted, for all his paranoia, did not seem to understand the *real* implication of Showalter's theorizing.

But as he stood and shot me a look, I saw – and I was not imagining it – the intent of Showalter's appearance in his eyes.

'Mr Bradshaw, I'll be in touch later today.' A good-neighbor smile. 'Sorry I got you all excited. I didn't mean to.'

A nod to me. 'See you again, I'm sure, Mr Conrad.'

When he was gone, Ted said, 'Can you believe that son of a bitch?'

I was in a hurry. 'Damn. I forgot to ask him about the ballistics.'

'Ballistics?'

'The kind of rifle and if they found the bullets.'

'Oh, yeah, right. The ballistics. I should've thought of that, too.'

'Let me see if I can catch him. I'll be right back.'

'Maybe I should go with you.'

'No, that's all right. You just sit here and relax now.'

I reached the hall in time to hear the massive front door click shut. I double-timed it to the front of the house. Showalter was moving at least as fast as I was. He was already standing next to his black Mercury. From the front porch, I said, 'Chief, I'd like to talk to you a minute.'

'Oh?'

I wanted to drown in the day. The scent of autumn in the hills, the soft soothing breezes, the burning colors of orange and gold and cocoa on the leaves, Churchill barking at birds. I did not want to approach Showalter and hear what I knew he would say. Not because I would believe it; the dread was that he already believed it.

I started out by telling him about the second call from the woman claiming to know about the shooting, and how I'd waited for her and her husband last night at the boat dock.

The smile was in no way convincing. 'You're a grown-up, Mr Conrad. You realize that you could be being played. That this is just some kind of prank.'

'I realize that.'

'If you feel guilty about not letting me know about your trip to the dock beforehand, don't. I appreciate that you didn't waste my time or the time of my officers.'

'Now let's talk about the real thing.'

'I'm not sure I'm following you, Mr Conrad.'

'Oh, I think you are. You danced all around it, but I picked up on what you were really saying.'

'And what was that?'

'That you don't think the attempted assassination was real.'

He paused; he was uncomfortable. 'Well, I don't think it was a serious attempt to kill the congresswoman.'

'I don't agree.'

'You can't *afford* to agree, Mr Conrad.'

So there we had it. He had just confirmed his real feelings.

'What you're really suggesting here is that we were behind the shooting.'

'One of the men on the task force brought it up this morning. Congresswoman Bradshaw was starting to lose in the polls – a one-point lead isn't much considering that she was several points ahead not long ago – and needed to turn things around.'

'You really think the congresswoman would have anything to do with staging an assassination attempt?'

'No, I don't. But that doesn't mean that somebody associated with her didn't stage it without her knowing.'

'So you're formally accusing us of staging the shooting?'

'No,' he said, opening his door. 'As I said inside, I'm just doing my job.' He slid behind the wheel. Just before he closed the door, he said, 'But it's a possibility.'

Then he was pulling abruptly away. Brisk, brusque, military.

Bastard.

PART TWO

FIFTEEN

'You're brooding,' Abby said.

This was much later in the afternoon.

'I have a damned good reason to brood.'

'Donna out front tells me that you've been brooding ever since you got back from Jess's this afternoon. She's very maternal toward me, Donna is, even though she's three years younger. She said, "Abby, I'm afraid if you go in there you'll start brooding, too. Whatever it is, it's serious." So how could I *not* come in here?'

'How'd the campaigning go the last couple of hours?'

'When we were at Wilson High School there were fourteen cops because there are so many ways into that place.'

I pointed to one of the chairs in front of the desk. She was wearing a matching green sweater and skirt. She must have needed a computer to keep track of the hearts she'd broken in high school and college. She had a prim way of sitting. She told me once that her mother had insisted that she take modeling classes even though full-grown Abby was five foot four. The modeling-class nonsense had stayed with her.

'Chief Showalter thinks that the assassination attempt was staged, Abby.'

'What the hell does that mean?'

'That the shooter wasn't really aiming at her.'

'So his shots went wild. That happens all the time. That doesn't mean it was "staged." And why would anybody "stage" it?' But she was bright, very bright, and realized the implication.

'We staged it because we were behind. We staged it to get sympathy.'

'Anybody who tried something like that would get nailed within a day or two.'

'We can't rule it out.'

'God, are you serious?' She seemed as shocked by my words as she had been when I'd told her about Showalter's. 'There's no way anybody on our staff—'

'It wouldn't have to be on our staff. It could be somebody on our staff who hired somebody—'

'You don't really believe that? You don't really agree with Showalter?'

'I don't agree with him and I'd sure as hell never admit to him something like that's possible. Those shots were so wild—'

I saw the first hint of doubt in those blue eyes I'd come to know so well. I was seeing in her what I was afraid I'd be seeing in the press very soon. That first instance of doubt, the shots having missed by so much.

I went back through my story about the mysterious phone caller. I told her Showalter believed it might be a prank.

But I always drew back from the prank theory. There was enough complicated anguish in her voice to make her real. The terrified wife who wanted to help her husband without getting the police involved. Which made no sense, but that was exactly the point. The panicked spouse whose plan made no sense.

But why hadn't she shown up last night? And why hadn't she at least called later to explain why she hadn't been able to make it?

'I think she's real, Dev. No matter what Showalter says.'

'So do I.'

'So that would eliminate both it being "staged" and anybody in our campaign being involved.'

'Probably.'

Even her frowns were cute. 'I just want a nice, simple, straight-forward assassination attempt we can ride all the way to a twenty-eight-point win on election day.'

'I take it you'd settle for a two-point win?'

'I'd settle for a point-four win.'

'I thought so.'

But our spurt of humor vanished as quickly as it had appeared. 'I need to find the woman,' I said.

'And just how do you plan to do that?'

'I know where to start, anyway. A place called the Skylight.'

'This is our secret, this conversation.'

'Of course.'

I was assuming that my GPS would take me to the Skylight tavern without any trouble. Last night the old man's 'GSP' reference had been funny. Within half an hour from now it would be anything but.

SIXTEEN

'd done some acting in college. A girl I'd been trying to get close to insisted I had 'the look.' I never did figure out what that meant exactly.

I didn't like acting much – and I was miserable at it – but I did get interested in the plays of Eugene O'Neill. I thought of him as I walked inside the Skylight tavern. The night man had come on at four. It was now four-twenty.

This was O'Neill turf, the land of lost souls. Every face in the place hinted at a story that would either break your heart or scare the shit out of you or both. Old, young, working class or homeless-looking needed – at a minimum – dentists, barbers and social workers.

The exceptions were the ex-military ones. Survivors of our many recent wars. The buzz cuts gave them away as well as the injuries: the man who played poker one-handed. The man with the left cheek burned into shallow ruts. The man in the wheelchair. The man with the missing ear and the black eyepatch.

There was no jukebox, just a TV set mounted upon the wall. It was turned off.

The customers hadn't shown much interest in me. The bartender, who was tall, bony and had a blue left eye that wandered, studied me as if I were an unknown species.

'What'll you have, mister?'

'You have Pepsi?'

'I'll have to charge you a buck.'

'That's all right.'

He flipped up a lid below the bar. Both arms bore faded tattoos signifying that he'd been in the U.S. Navy. I guessed he'd served on a ship during Vietnam.

A radio turned low vibrated with the sounds of a baseball game. No wonder he hadn't been interested when I'd walked in. This year the playoffs for the World Series were as exciting as any in the last decade.

He nodded his knobby bald head to the TV set above us. 'I'd rather watch it but you know how much those bastards want to come out here and fix it? Hell, it ain't more than ten years old or so.'

I thought of all the technological developments in the last ten years. If cavemen had had TV sets they would have been identical to the heavy box perched above us. But the kind of money he probably made in a place like this precluded him from most extra expenses. And this particular group of men seemed more interested in their conversations than anything else. I was sure that men in dungeons had talked a lot, too.

'Not much sense in fixin' it, anyway,' he said. 'City council's all set to tear this place down. We're one of the few places standin'.'

He was right about that. The Godzillas of urban renewal had leveled a few square miles of this area. Piles of rubble lay on blocks of empty dirt lots. Between medical facilities, parking lots and mini-malls, land was at a premium in Danton.

'Most of the guys in here grew up in the neighborhood. They come back here 'cause their dads and their granddads came here.'

He'd turned out, surprisingly, to be a talker.

And then I saw him. I had to stare to make sure. He stopped and spoke to the men at one of the tables. He must have said something funny. For a man who was right on the verge of being dumped in an old folks' home, he was a sprightly son of a bitch. Even a bit jaunty.

He took a stool at the end of the bar. A few more hellos to the regulars talking and paying half-assed attention to the game. His eyes had yet to travel down to where I sat.

I'd been about to ask the bartender all about a certain female customer of his delivered here by cab the night before last, but now a more interesting possibility had presented itself.

And he saw me. He was cooler about it than I would have expected. He even started talking to the Hispanic man seated next to him. He kept glancing up. Couldn't resist. He knew that unless he did something, and fast, he would have to face me. And answer a lot of uncomfortable questions.

Then, he bolted. No warning.

He wasn't as old and infirm as he'd pretended to be last night, but he wasn't young and there was a stiffness – maybe soreness – in the legs he was pushing much faster than they wanted to be pushed.

I almost tripped across the threshold as I ran after him. The sunlight blinded me momentarily as I looked around for him.

He stood at the same newer Ford he'd been in last night. But his run must have tired him because as he stood trying to unlock his car his entire body heaved with the effort.

I clamped my hand on his bony shoulder and spun him around. In the daylight the face, for all its wrinkles, was livelier than it had been when he'd been pretending to be nearing dementia. Now the brown gaze was wilier. He glanced at his Ford. I'd already memorized the license number.

'How's your GSP doing?'

'I don't have to talk to you.' His faded yellow sports shirt was soaked with sweat; his face gleamed.

'You don't have to, but you will. And right now.'

'You don't cut shit with me.' But he was gasping as he said this.

'I may not. But the police will.'

The jaws tensed. 'I ain't afraid of cops.'

'Good for you. I am.'

He was looking past my shoulder. Even without turning around I knew that he was looking for a savior.

I looked back at the busted concrete steps leading into the tavern. He'd got two-for-one saviors, a pair of hefty guys who might be well into middle age but could still bust heads without any difficulty.

'Over here, Billy. This asshole is givin' me grief.'

But the other one, in a faded Levi's long-sleeved shirt, said, 'Hang on, Frank.'

'Thanks, Sonny.' Then to me, 'Now you'll get it.'

They kept their arms wide of their torsos the way movies and TV taught us the old gunfighters did. Then they pasted on their best psychopath smiles as they started down the steps. Billy went up on the moment by stumbling into one of the cracks on the concrete steps. He fell against Sonny, who pushed him off as if his buddy was carrying at least cooties, if not leprosy.

Now that they were on the pavement they squared their shoulders, readjusted their gunfighter stances and walked over to us.

'You givin' Frank a problem, man?' This close Billy smelled of cloying beer, cigarettes and sweat. He was ready. His hands were fists. Sizable fists.

'Frank's an old dude,' Sonny said. He'd recently run through the place where they sprayed you with Aqua Velva for four or five minutes. 'Have to be a real chicken-shit motherfucker to pick on an old dude.' He nodded, not to Frank but to Billy. They'd had this act going since second grade.

'The police would like to talk to him.'

'And you're the cops, huh?'

'No.'

'No?' A Billy-to-Sonny glance. 'And here I was all ready to bow.'

Sonny obliged with a chuckle.

'He's got me confused with somebody else, Billy. That's why he's hasslin' me.'

'Who's he think you are?' Sonny said.

Three enormous dump trucks boomed past. We stood silent like children in awe of all mobile and metal things that big.

Apparently Billy had had time to figure out a solution to Frank's dilemma. 'You wanna get in your car and drive away, Frank?'

'You bet I do. But he won't let me.'

'This asshole, you mean?'

'Yeah.'

Sonny did a little acting. He shook his head as if he'd just been told that I'd set fire to a children's ward. 'Well, that kind of bullshit ain't gonna stand, Frank. You wanna get in your car'n drive away, that's your business.'

'You fuckin' right it is.'

Billy and Sonny had taken several steps closer to me. They had also separated so they could, if necessary, come at me from both sides.

'Frank,' Sonny said, 'you get in your car, start it up and go home or wherever you want to go.'

'What if he follows me, Sonny?'

His smile was a shiv. 'Oh, he won't be followin' you. We'll see to that.'

'I really appreciate this, boys. You know I'm not in the best of health and then to have some slick bastard like this get on my case—'

'Go, Frank,' Billy said, 'and be sure to say hello to Cindy for me.'

Frank's wince told me that Billy shouldn't have used the name 'Cindy' – or 'Frank,' for that matter. I had the license number and two names. Unless his two friends decided to crack a few of my ribs, I was satisfied with this trip.

Frank managed to drop his keys as he tried to unlock the Ford. No, he wasn't as helpless as he'd pretended to be last night, but he was not in good shape. He almost pitched over as he retrieved them.

The three of us watched him get his car going and drive away.

'So who're you supposed to be?' Billy said.

'I work for Congresswoman Bradshaw.'

'That bitch,' Sonny said. 'She's a socialist, for one thing, and she wants to teach little kids a load of bullshit about our country.'

'And she likes fags.'

'So what the hell are you botherin' old Frank for?'

'I can't say.'

'He can't say.' They were doing their road show act again. Bouncing lines off each other and grinning.

'Because he's important. That's why he can't say.'

'He works for Bradshaw. And he admits it.'

I guess you'd call it a chortle. They traded them back and forth.

'I'm going now.'

'You go when we say so.'

'I'm betting you've got some kind of criminal record, asshole,' I said to Billy. 'You're holding me against my will. And I've got the kind of lawyer who'd love to put you away for a long time. Both of you.'

Sonny moved on me. But he was out of shape and a brawler rather than a fighter. He swung so wide at my head that I was able to use his considerable belly to plant my fist so deep I wondered if I'd be able to yank it back out.

He stumbled, dropped to his knees and started the kind of gagging that meant he'd soon enough be puking.

Fascinating as the prospect of watching it was, I decided that now would be a good time to leave.

SEVENTEEN

I called a friend of mine in the Chicago Police Department. I'd needed him for several different jobs in the past and paid him so well for them that he'd usually oblige me. I gave him Frank's license plate and asked him if he'd run it for me. Hopefully the computer would yield a viable address.

I spent half an hour checking out the internals from our other campaigns. A couple of calls were warranted. I always feel that I owe my associates civility and the benefit of the doubt. I only get argumentative when one of them tries to evade responsibility for a mistake, or worse, tries to blame it on someone else. All I want to do is solve the problem, not denigrate somebody. My final call was to Ted.

'I'm still pissed about Showalter this morning, Dev.'

I decided against upsetting him even more. 'I'm just checking in to see how Jess is doing.'

'She's really up for the fundraiser tonight. She even had her hairdresser come out here this afternoon.'

'You didn't mention anything to her about this "staged" business, did you?'

'Hell, no. That'd be all she needed to hear. She'll be having nightmares about it the rest of her life. And then some asshole police chief—'

'I'll do my best to make it tonight, Ted. But there's a good chance I'll be busy working.'

'You're kidding. People always want to meet you, Dev. Especially the important people. They know your track record, so they're impressed.'

'I'll do what I can, Ted. Give my love to Jess. Right now I need to go.'

'I just hope you're there. You and Jess are the stars.'

Ted's flattery was amusing. I'd managed to talk the director into letting Ted wear his black turtleneck and I'd sided with Ted against Showalter. For at least a few more hours I'd be in the Wonderful Guy category.

I peeked into Abby's office to see if she'd join me for a pizza down the street but, like the rest of the staff, she'd gone. Those salmon-colored clouds were in the windows again. I had too many things grinding on me to get my usual dusk depression.

I'd just gotten back from the john when the phone rang. It was my Chicago P.D. friend. The man was Frank Grimes. Age 71. Retired. 2731 36th Street Southwest, Danton.

I didn't have any specific reason to link Grimes and my mystery caller, but the more I thought about last night, the more his sudden appearance out at the dock seemed less and less coincidental. And then he'd tried to run away when he saw me today. I needed to find out a lot more about Frank Grimes.

The area was mixed race and tumbledown.

At twenty minutes after seven a sparse number of yellowish street lights revealed the disrepair of the homes and even of the corner gas station and drugstore. The houses and the businesses were tightly packed and busted up both by time and the kind of battering rendered by the teenagers who'd lived here. The music, the clothes and the slang might have changed over the years but the contempt of the young men and women for the debris and rubble of the place had not. They knew it was a shithole; why not make it even more so?

Grimes's Ford was parked at the curb. The address it belonged to was typical of the meager houses so prevalent here. A very slanted roof covered a gray stucco one-story home. A long piece of tape covered the crack in the lighted front window. The metal railing on the three front steps leaned so far backward it appeared ready to fall off. A push lawnmower stood in the center of the miniature front lawn. Unlike the other midget lawns nearby, this one was clean of beer cans and scraps of paper.

The street was busy with open-windowed cars blasting both rap and country music. A number of the cars had the kind of mufflers that rumbled. A pair of very young teenage girls in tight jeans and even tighter sweaters strolled down the sidewalk on my side of the street. They were almost comically conscious of the admiring looks, shouts and horn blasts of the boys cruising past. They were babes all right, but in this neighborhood they wouldn't be babes for long. Pregnancy, drugs or husbands with mean intent would make them old and sad before they reached twenty.

I locked the car and walked to the porch. The wood beneath me was weak with age.

The colored lights of a TV screen played on the taped window. From what I could gather it was a crime show of some kind. The music was the tip-off.

I knocked. No responding sound. The TV volume stayed the same, no footsteps on the floor inside and no voice acknowledging the knock.

This time I knocked much harder – three times.

When I didn't get any response, I stepped up to the window and peeked in.

The order and neatness of the living room triumphed over the worn and threadbare furnishings. Framed faded photographs lined the wall above the couch with the flowery slipcovers. I counted twelve, thirteen, fourteen framed photos of the same woman at various ages. I was sure there would be others throughout the house.

Lying in front of the swaybacked couch was Frank Grimes. Somebody using something had struck him in the forehead. He now lay face-up with a massive purple wound above his left eye.

'Who're you?'

A female voice from behind me. Because of the shadowy street-light I couldn't see much of her. Long blonde hair, an angular face, a slender, tall body in a Levi's jacket, white blouse and jeans. Oh – and a handgun.

'Did you hear me? I asked who you are.'

I took a chance. 'I'm the guy you've been calling. Dev Conrad.'

'Oh, my God.' She seemed to forget she was the one holding the gun. But any authority the gun had given had faded when I told her my name. 'How did you find me?'

'I found Frank, and that led me to you. And speaking of Frank, he's not in very good shape right now. He's lying on the floor in there with a bad wound on his forehead.'

'What? Oh, God, poor Granddad!'

She ran straight up the steps, brushing past me to get to the door. 'Here,' she said, 'hold this,' and jammed the gun into my hand. It was the latest version of a single-action, semi-automatic Browning that had been used in all our wars, starting with WWI.

She dropped the house key and had to scramble for it in the dark. In the meantime, she yelled, 'Granddad! Granddad!'

She was so disturbed I had to find the key for her. She got it in the lock, slammed the door inward and went straight to him. The way she checked his vitals indicated that she'd had at least minimal medical training of some kind.

'Please help me get him on the couch. He has terrible heart problems. He's lucky to be alive.'

He was heavier than I would have thought. Just before we laid him carefully on the cheap, ruined couch his eyes opened and he groaned.

Once we got his body lying flat and straight she plucked a throw pillow from a nearby tattered armchair and set it under his head.

'Watch him. I'll be right back.'

He was hurt, no doubt about it, but not hurt enough to be civil. 'What the hell are you doin' here?'

'You know who did this to you?'

He moved his head faster than was wise and paid for it. His face cramped with pain. He grumbled and then cursed. 'You son of a bitch. I asked you a question. What the hell're you doing here?'

'I've been looking for you.'

'Well, don't. You're a stupid bastard.' A cringe; he'd moved his head abruptly again. 'You're getting into something you don't understand and you're going to get somebody killed.'

Cindy was back with an official-looking white first-aid kit. 'I'm a nurse.' She said this as she brushed me aside. She was getting good at it. First on the porch and now as I stood by the couch. Apparently I was a piece of human furniture.

As she hunched down to begin her examination, she glanced up at me with a freckled Midwestern-girl face that was a little too spare to be pretty but had a friendly, intelligent appeal to the dark eyes and full mouth.

I got the job of holding the flashlight and beaming it at the wound while she examined it.

'Do you have a headache?'

'Do I have a headache? Of course I have a headache, honey.'

She had brought along a cup of hot water and a clean cloth. She cleaned the wound – a deep horizontal gash about the length of his eyebrow – and examined his eyes for signs of a concussion. Then she used an antiseptic on the trauma area.

'We'll need to get this stitched up.'

'Oh, no, honey, you're not getting me in any hospital.'

'He's terrified of hospitals, Mr Conrad.'

'I had too many friends die in them after Nam.'

'That's because they'd been seriously wounded, Granddad. We'll just go to the ER.'

'The ER is the hospital.'

'It's part of the hospital but for a few stitches they won't admit you. Now be quiet and let me finish my work.'

She made him take two aspirin, which he objected to. And she took his temperature for a second time, which he also objected to.

'You're a terrible patient, Granddad.'

'Aw, honey, you know I love you and I appreciate all your concern. It's just all this medical stuff scares me. You know that.' The tenderness in his voice came as a shock.

'Now we have to sit up and go to the hospital.'

'I have a big car,' I said. 'You can sit in the backseat with him while I drive.'

'Oh, no, I don't want nothin' to do with him and you shouldn't either, honey. He just wants to get you alone so he can ask you a bunch of questions.'

'I need to know who hit you and you know why he hit you. You're holding back and I don't know why. I'm trying to help you.'

'See what I'm saying?' he shouted.

She was standing now and looking at me. 'Well, I think I do owe him some sort of explanation, Granddad. So c'mon, let's let him give us a ride to the ER.'

EIGHTEEN

No wives or girlfriends beaten badly, no drunks injured in tavern fights, no victims of car or motorcycle accidents. These would appear later. It was not quite eight-thirty and the patients in the ER ran to kids with broken fingers, arms and ankles, and elderly patients suffering from age.

The large white room with as many as twenty-five colored plastic chairs for patients had an empty feeling, in fact. No crying babies, no sobbing wives, no drunks escorted by police officers.

After the paperwork was finished Frank Grimes was immediately taken to a room down the hall. So we sat there among the antiseptic smells and the constant ringing of phones and the techs who brought patients back to their loved ones, and for the first time Cindy told me about herself and her situation.

Her husband's name was Dave Fletcher. He'd dropped out of the local community college – he'd planned to have his own landscaping business – after a friend of his convinced him to join the army and head to the Middle East. She said that she'd always resented the influence his best friends had on him. She'd been so angry about his dropping out of community college and willingly putting himself in war that she'd packed up and left two weeks before he was shipped overseas. He'd called or emailed every chance he got from boot camp. She'd answer him but didn't forgive him.

During his second tour she'd divorced him and lived with a young doctor from the hospital where she worked. She'd never agree to marry him and so he finally started dating another nurse. It was in the first month of Dave's third tour that he was shot in the head in a firefight. He was in a coma for months and not expected to live. But he did live and returned – against all odds – to reasonably good physical health. His mental health was another matter.

He'd lived with his folks; depression and suicidal impulses kept him seeing his VA shrink three times a month. Eventually she called him and they'd ended up talking for almost two hours. She'd realized that she still loved him and probably always would. They had remarried less than two months after their long phone call.

Despite some incidents with Dave's former psychological problems, she'd loved being with him again. And for the first time they'd begun talking about having a kid or two.

Dave had a friend on the Danton police force. He'd introduced him to Police Chief Showalter and Showalter liked Dave enough that he waived Dave's psychological problems and put him in uniform and on the street. Cindy said that while there were some good cops in a river town where the casino was a major employer you got the kind of cops you might expect.

Unfortunately, Dave had gotten involved with three or four cops who shared the racist and anti-government opinions he'd picked up in the military. The only thing she could compare it to was a religious conversion. He'd fixed up their basement as a kind of headquarters, the walls covered with ugly racist and anti-government posters. He'd started buying expensive guns.

Not even her announcement that she was pregnant had excited him the way group meetings did.

The ones who came to the house were always talking about 'the revolution' and 'when we start shooting.' At first she'd thought they were just living out a fantasy. All dressed up in military gear some-times, always ready with violent threats against the government. Almost as bad, she said, was the cop bar where Dave spent way too much time. 'Batter Up,' it was called.

She'd lost the baby five months in. She'd been having vaginal bleeding and abdominal cramping and then suddenly she hadn't been able to feel the baby moving inside her anymore. Following the loss of the child, Dave had surprised her by being the man she'd married. He'd been tender, attentive, even lying on the bed one night and holding her. Even crying himself as they'd talked about what might have been.

But their closeness had faded as he'd drifted back into the group again. He'd told her that wives and girlfriends also participated, but she'd liked nothing about his friends.

She noted that he'd been having stress headaches and fits of anger and depression in the last three weeks. Obviously something was going on but he wouldn't talk about it.

And then, the night before last, he'd called and said he had to leave town. He'd sounded clinically insane to her. Agitated and fearful. He'd started crying.

'He said he'd done something he shouldn't have. Something big. And then he said that he'd made a recording on this little digital recorder he always carried. It fits right in his pocket.'

'What kind of recording?'

'Something that would expose everything about the things his group had done. I tried to keep him on the phone because I was so worried about him. But he hung up and I couldn't stop him. I was terrified.'

After she learned about Jess being fired on she wondered if Dave had had anything to do with it. As did her granddad. She'd seen me interviewed on TV as Jess's campaign manager. She called all the hotels to find out where I was staying. She went to my hotel but then got scared and ran off. She wondered if she'd find Dave at the Skylight, a local hangout, which is why she went there. She set up the meeting with me at the boat dock but when her granddad heard about it he'd insisted on checking me out.

'So who do you think hit him tonight?'

'I'm not sure.'

'It could've been Dave.'

'He wouldn't hurt my granddad. He knows how much I love him.'

'You said yourself that Dave sounded insane.'

'No, no it couldn't have been him.' Then, 'Granddad's so lonely. He never got over my grandmother's death. He's got all those photos of her all over the house and now he's a big-time Catholic again. He goes to Mass three times a week.'

A nurse brought Grimes over to us. He had a long, narrow piece of white plastic over the wound.

'We checked him carefully. We don't see any problem except for the wound. And that will heal itself. But if you notice anything else, Cindy—' The nurse smiled. 'Well, you know the drill.'

'Thanks, Louise.'

Louise turned around and headed back to the examination rooms.

'You have any idea how long I was back there?' Grimes was back to his squawking again.

'Long enough for me to tell Dev a story he probably found very dull.'

'It was very helpful, Cindy.'

'So you told him everything, huh?' He said this loudly and bitterly enough to attract the attention of half the ER people.

She slid her arm through his. 'C'mon now, Granddad. Let's get you home.'

NINETEEN

I can't say they were happy to see me walk into Batter Up.

Some of them were too deep in conversation, too deep in bumper pool and too deep in a ball game on TV to pay any attention. They would have been just as unhappy as the others if they'd noticed me.

Outwardly I was like a good number of them. White, fortyish, clean-cut. But in places like this that wasn't enough. No, it certainly was not.

This was Danton's one and only police bar.

Housed in an elderly brick building, windows painted black, the interior narrow with a long bar running half the length of the west wall and the rest of the space divided up into six red leathered booths and four tiny tables, the place was worn but scrupulously clean. The east walls were covered with a large American flag and posters for the Chicago Bears and the University of Illinois football and basketball teams. Set off on their own were large framed photos of officers who'd died in the line of duty, and as a final touch, as if to annoy me especially, a huge campaign poster of Dorsey.

There were three or four couples here and they all sat at tables. The women were young and sexual and looked to be having a good time, at least if their high, happy laughter was any indication. They were girlfriends and maybe cop groupies. The exception was an older couple, who sat in silence and stared at each other. He looked angry and she looked sunk in gray despair. Maybe they were splitting up after years of marriage; maybe one of their kids had become a problem. Given the merry human noise and the country-western noise on the jukebox, they didn't belong here.

The bartender was short and wide, maybe fifty, and muscular in a way his short-sleeved red shirt only emphasized. A convict who worked out every day for three years would have envied him. He also had a pair of eyes that could spit their contempt at you.

'I get the feeling you don't belong here, which means I don't *want* you here.' Short, blunt fingers on his left hand touched the swollen bicep on his right arm.

'I'm looking for Dave Fletcher.'

'I bet he's not looking for you.'

'Mind if I ask around?'

'Why?'

'As I said, I'm looking for him. Personal reason.'

Over the years I'd been in maybe a dozen cop bars. They weren't always happy to have civilian visitors, but this kind of contempt and mistrust was new for me. I didn't like to admit that it was intimidating, but I didn't have much choice.

The bartender had a unique way of communicating with his

customers. He took out a ball bat and banged it on the bar. He had to do this a couple of times before he got the amount of attention he wanted. He had some kind of long black remote in his free hand. He used it to mute the jukebox.

'Guy here is looking for Dave Fletcher.'

Somebody shouted: 'You know who he is?'

'Uh-uh.'

'Saw his picture in the paper the other day. He's some kind of mucky-muck in the Bradshaw campaign.'

Somebody laughed. 'Dude, you picked the wrong place.'

He got the response he wanted. Hilarity ensued.

I was now not so much a villain as a feckless clown. The bartender poked me in the back. Baseball bats are good for multitasking.

'Think you better get the hell out of here, buddy.'

I took a last shot. 'So none of you have seen him?'

This time the bat didn't poke me. It slammed against my spine. 'Get out of here, asshole. And right now.'

Even the older woman in despair looked appreciative for the distraction. She watched with great fascination. Unfortunately I'd left my Rambo kit at home.

I just started walking to the front door.

'Maybe you didn't notice, jerk-off. We're all voting for Dorsey.'

Another wag got another collective laugh but by then I was at the door and pushing into the smoky-smelling chill of the autumn night. I'd had to park on the next long block. The bar had only a tiny parking lot so most customers had to use the curb.

The voice was friendly enough. I didn't worry about one of the bar denizens wanting to fight me. I heard it when I was just a few feet from my car. This neighborhood had been deserted for some time. Dirty words on walls and windows were so obvious you couldn't even dignify them with the term graffiti. Graffiti could be clever, even artful, at times.

I did take the precaution of turning around and setting myself for a fight. And if it did come – if I had misinterpreted the tenor of that voice – then I was going to start throwing punches with maniacal fury. The embarrassment of the cop bar scene still stung.

He was running in the dark. When he reached me he was bathed in the dirty streetlight of this dirty, half-deserted neighborhood.

'Hey, man, I'm sorry about Henry. He's an asshole. I hate the bastard. I took my brother there one night and he treated him like hell.' All this came out between gasps.

I recognized him as one of the young ones along the bar. Curly dark hair, slim, dark V-neck sweater, jeans and white running shoes. Right now he was out of breath. He might be young and slender but he wasn't in great shape.

'Just give me a second, OK?'

I relaxed for the first time since I'd pushed open the door to the cop bar.

'I—' He waved me off and then began taking deep breaths. 'My name's Andy Bromfield. I saw Dave last night. He was—' One more deep breath. 'I just saw him for a couple of minutes at this convenience store. We live in the same neighborhood. He was pretty messed up. Scared and kind of babbling. He was like that when he first got back from Afghanistan. I couldn't figure out what he was talking about. We were high-school buddies. I tried to call Cindy but I didn't get any answer. I was worried about him.'

'So you didn't have any idea where he was going?'

'No. Like I said, he just seemed confused.' Then, 'Sorry about the bar back there. Most of the guys are pretty decent most of the time – when strangers come in, I mean. The ones who gave you shit were in Showalter's little group. They don't like strangers. Hell, they don't even like the rest of us that much. They hang out together. Terrible way to run a police force, if you ask me.'

'Dave Fletcher's in the group, isn't he?'

'Yeah. But lately he's been talking to me a lot more about the old days, when we hung out in high school and stuff. There was a while there when he acted like he didn't want anything to do with me. The others are still like that. Like they have their own little police force.'

'You ever think of quitting?'

'The wife just had baby number three. We're kind of tied down right now. The only other thing I might consider is working at the casino being a dealer or something. They make pretty good money for the area.' He seemed amused now. 'Of course, the whole place is for shit. This is like some little redneck town where I grew up in Arkansas. That's why I was comfortable here at first. But no more. The wife had two years of college and she thinks this is strictly Hicksville.'

This wasn't getting me the kind of information I needed.

'Any idea where Dave might go?'

'I guess he's not at home, huh?'

'No.'

'Figures.'

'Why's that?'

'The wife and Cindy are friends. Cindy won't come right out and say it, but Molly says she gets the idea that they've been having some pretty bad marriage problems. Cindy hates his little group.' Then, 'If he still has that old trailer of his, you might try there.'

'He has a trailer?'

'Yeah. He has an uncle who owns some property out in the country. Maybe ten acres is all. There's this old trailer on it. An old silver one. We always used that as a hangout in high school. Take girls out there and drink beer and get laid if we got lucky. Damned thing is falling apart by now, I'm sure, but knowing Dave he probably hasn't given up on it.'

'Could you give me directions?'

'Sure,' he said. He made them as simple as possible. Then he said, 'Sorry again about all the hassle in the bar.'

'Yeah,' I said, 'give that bartender my best.'

TWENTY

Somebody was following me.

Dark green van of relatively recent vintage.

I spotted it when the traffic thinned on four different occasions during my trek into the country. The first two times he was three cars behind me. The third time he was two cars behind me. The fourth time he was four cars behind me.

But he was cleverer than I thought. The closer I got to my destination the more often he disappeared. Maybe he was from the cop bar and had followed me from there. Or maybe because I'd asked about Dave Fletcher he knew where I'd look. I mean, it was obvious I was going into the country, and if he knew Dave he knew about Dave's trailer, and if he knew about Dave's trailer, he'd know by now where I was going. He'd just hang back and then show up when he chose.

To reach Dave Fletcher's trailer you followed a narrow, deeply rutted dirt road that paralleled a long stretch of woods. The farmland had been posted but it was doubtful his uncle was sitting around with his sawed-off shotgun waiting for trespassers.

It was another autumn night with a full moon that mourned us all, but in an oddly elegant way, like a lovely but sad song. Just inside the gate a carefully arranged line of fiercely orange pumpkins sat by an old faded pickup truck with a MONDALE FOR PRESIDENT sticker on the rear bumper. All we needed was a scarecrow.

What confronted me was little more than a trail. If you drove faster than ten miles per hour your car turned into a carnival ride. You could crack your skull on the roof.

About a quarter mile past this in a shallow valley a forlorn mutt of impressive size crouched next to a large boulder. He chose to run away when he saw me. Maybe twenty yards from him stood one of those venerable aluminum Airstream trailers that might well date back six or seven decades. The damned things lasted.

Just as I was leaving my car and making my way to the Airstream I heard a motor come to a stop on the road behind me. There was a windbreak about a city block from the gate making it difficult to see the road.

I always packed a utility flashlight in any vehicle I was driving. I wished I'd brought a more powerful one for tonight. I swung the light back and forth over the brown dead grass that had been used as a dumping ground for everything from beer cans to a white pair of women's panties.

Another noise from somewhere on the road jostled me. I gaped behind to see a sedan of some kind driving faster than it should have eastward.

I'd gotten spooked because I was afraid I'd find Dave in the trailer. I'd been around my share of dead people before. It's never exactly your preferred source of entertainment but you become accustomed to the look and various shapes and stenches of corpses.

No, my worry was that if I found him I'd have to call Cindy and tell her. And that I wasn't up to.

Before going into the Airstream I took a paranoid look in all directions. There was a farmhouse but it was a good quarter mile away. There was a silo and another farmhouse in the opposite direction at about the same distance. Behind the Airstream was a line of pines and the sound of the river. Then I spent a few minutes studying the road.

There was wind and a hint of cold rain and somewhere in the gathering clouds was the sound of a passenger jet.

Isolation.

Or maybe not.

He could be anywhere, the driver of the van.

He could have field glasses on me right now. Or, if he was familiar with the property, he could have swung wide and hidden himself in the pines behind the Airstream.

The Glock was stuffed into my belt. But not even the Glock comforted me when I realized that the trailer wasn't locked. Not a good sign. There was a small window on the right side of the door. I went up to it and shone my light inside.

My first impression was that the small interior had been tossed. Somebody had been looking frantically for something. But as I followed the beam I realized that, no, this was just the way some men lived. No mom, no wifey around, what the hell.

I saw a crusted pizza box with a sock resting on it. A men's magazine open to a page of a young woman pleasuring herself with a vibrator. A tiny table overflowing with beer cans and bottles. A rusty basin on another tiny table with dirty scabbed dishes mounted high in it. Clothes strewn everywhere. More beer cans and bottles forming minefields for anybody moving around in the dark, especially if they were drunk. Sections of newspaper had been flung across a ripped mini-couch and there were numerous sacks from Hardee's, McDonald's, Burger King and others.

Paradise.

I probably wouldn't have to call Cindy tonight unless it was to tell her that her husband was on track to be in the Slob Hall of Fame, but she probably already knew that.

I went inside, still wondering why Dave would have left the trailer unlocked.

No need to mention that the place stank.

No need to mention that I had to be careful not to lodge my foot on a beer bottle and go sailing away.

No need to mention that in this diminutive garbage can there was no body. My flashlight check through the window had pretty much guaranteed me of that.

The most important thing I hadn't seen through the window was a stack of reprinted articles on the floor that mostly concerned overthrowing the government. Several of them were illustrated with photographs of various kinds of automated weaponry.

But . . . nothing.

I looked for evidence that he'd been here recently but I didn't find it. All the dead cigarette butts told me that he was a heavy smoker but not even the smoke smelled fresh.

A wasted trip.

Fatigue set in, as if a switch had been flipped.

I went outside, greeting the night air and the mournful moon.

I started walking back to my car and, as I did so, I saw somebody just clear the sizable boulder and start running away in the direction of the road.

She was definitely fast. *She*.

I knew I couldn't catch her but I started running anyway. And there, in the moonlight, she made the mistake of looking over her shoulder.

Black jeans, black crew-neck sweater.

Running.

In that moment when she turned so I could glimpse her face, I saw who she was. Showalter's eye candy. Karen Foster.

Not long after I heard the van engine start and she was gone.

TWENTY-ONE

I had breakfast in my office, my usual bagel with cream cheese and black coffee.

I'd gotten there early so I could spend an hour catching up on my shop's other campaigns. No surprises, which was good news for some and bad news for others. Nationally, my party was looking bad in four key states. There was a danger we could lose the Senate.

I tried not to think about that particular piece of bad news. But that was just a prelude. The *real* bad news came when I stumbled across a bulletin on the local newspaper's website. *Police Chief Aaron Showalter will hold a televised press conference at 10.30 this morning.*

Abby also got in early, as usual. She said, 'I can see by your frown that you've heard what Showalter's up to.'

'We need to stay calm. I have cyanide capsules for both of us if he turns on us.'

'Well, just give me mine now.'

I had one large bite of my bagel left. She picked it up and ate it. 'My buddy at Channel 3 says two different reporters want to pick up on the "staged" thing but that the news director won't let them until there's some kind of proof.'

I then told her about Cindy Fletcher and Grimes.

'Line two, Dev. It's Ted Bradshaw and he sounds upset.'

'Gosh,' I said to Abby. 'Ted Bradshaw upset? Life is just full of surprises.'

He bellered into the phone, 'Have you heard about this fucking press conference?'

The blue suit looked new, the hair had been cut and the body language was somewhat more studied and dramatic. TV can control you or you can control it. Somewhere along the line Showalter had learned that immortal truth.

He stood in front of a podium covered with media microphones. The setting was the large marble central floor of the county court-house. Then the press conference started.

Showalter: 'I apologize for not holding this press conference sooner, but as you can imagine, the task force has been busy. We worked till nearly one o'clock this morning.'

Reporter One: 'The big question we all want to ask is why you think the assassin's – or would-be assassin's – bullets went so wild? He wasn't that far away, and from the ballistics report the task force put out, he used a powerful rifle. Do you think he just got scared?'

Showalter: 'We can't *know* why they went wild. There's certainly the possibility that at the last minute he got spooked by what he was going to do. There's also the possibility that he was an amateur and that he had a lot of anger but not a lot of skill.'

Reporter Two: 'How about the possibility that he just wanted to scare her?'

Showalter: 'That's certainly a possibility, too.'

Reporter Three: 'How about the possibility that it was staged by somebody on Congresswoman Bradshaw's staff to win sympathy for her?'

For the first time, Showalter showed discomfort. He paused at least three or four seconds before he spoke.

Showalter: 'At nine-fifteen this morning, after we received an anonymous tip, Detective Michaels and Detective Donlon obtained a search warrant from Judge Sandra Windom to search the premises and the automobile of Cortland Thomas Tucker. Because he lives with his parents we made a point of securing their permission as well. Mr Tucker is a volunteer driver for the Bradshaw campaign.'

Reporter Four: 'Have they questioned him yet?'

Abby and I were alone in my office watching on my computer. From the reception area I heard two or three people talking back loudly, angrily to the screen they were watching. No way was Cory Tucker guilty of anything. One of the women sounded as if she was about to start crying.

The only thing Abby said was, 'I don't believe any of this.'

I nodded.

Showalter: 'Mr Tucker is being questioned right now. We will likely release the statements this afternoon.'

Reporter Five: 'Was there any physical evidence found?'

Showalter: 'All I can say is that we feel something important was found in the trunk of Mr Tucker's car. We haven't had time to assess it at any length. Most likely we'll address an entire range of questions in our written statements this afternoon.'

Reporter Six: 'Have you contacted anybody in the Bradshaw campaign?'

Showalter: 'No.'

Reporter Seven: 'So Tucker has not admitted to anything?'

Showalter smiled. 'Maybe you could call the police station and ask for interrogation room three. That's where they're questioning Mr Tucker right now. A detective will answer. You can ask him.'

The press loved the humor.

The phone rang. I didn't need to use my legendary psychic powers to know who'd be calling me. Jess or Ted. I was hoping Jess.

'Hi, Dev. Please tell me you don't believe Cory had anything to do with this.'

'He didn't, Jess. Somebody set him up.'

'That happens in real life, not just on TV?'

'It happens a lot.'

'Now if I can just stop my heart from racing at three thousand miles an hour.'

'Showalter didn't give you any kind of warning?'

'None.'

'I'm turning the campaign over to Abby. I want to work on this myself.'

'I want to call Cory's parents and tell them that he'll have the best lawyers and the best detectives working to exonerate him.'

'Let me call Mike Edelstein in Chicago. This'll be so high profile he'll be out here in a few hours.'

'All right. That's what I'll tell Cory's folks.' Then, 'Could Dorsey be behind this, Dev? I hate to think that. That's the first thing we all thought of here. Ted and me, I mean.'

'I hate to think so, too.'

'The hate mail we get – it could be any of them.'

'You're sure right about that.'

'Well, I'd better go. Please have Abby call me right away. Do you think we should keep to our schedule today? I'm supposed to visit three different places.'

'It's your call, Jess. The press'll be all over you. It could get ugly.'

'But you'd like me to go anyway, wouldn't you, Dev?'

'I'm not the one who has to face a press that'll already be convinced that Cory's guilty and that you and I and Ted were behind the whole thing.'

'It's so infuriating.'

'That's why I want to get working on it. I'll have Abby call you.'

'You're aware that I'm going to keep all our appearances today, aren't you?'

'There was never any question in my mind, Jess.'

The gentle laugh contrasted with the harsh facts facing us. 'Thank you for saying that, Dev. Thank you very much.'

TWENTY-TWO

Over the years I'd had to bail three or four of my politicians out of jail – and during my army days I'd interrogated more than a few prisoners in civil jails – but I'd never before had to seek to see somebody being held on a half-million-dollar bond.

We were three hours out from Showalter's press conference but, as I climbed the police station's front steps, his words still played in my mind.

The female officer at the reception desk, once I'd given her my name and asked to see Cory, said, 'I don't think that's possible – you're not his lawyer.'

'He works for me.' A lie, but what the hell. God had personally given me a daily allotment of one hundred and twenty-three lies. I was, after all, in politics.

She might not be pounding a beat but she was all cop. She fixed me with a pirate's cynical eye and said, 'He worked for you?'

'Yes. He was my driver. I'm with the Bradshaw campaign.'

'I see. But that still doesn't make any difference. He's been charged.'

'Right now we're waiting for his lawyer to get here from Chicago.'

'He doesn't have a local lawyer?'

'No.'

'Huh,' she said. But it wasn't a good 'huh.' It was, in fact, a very bad 'huh.' *Bringing in a lawyer from Chicago. He's so guilty one of the local lawyers could never do the job. And this guy, this Conrad here, looks like* he's *from Chicago now that I think about it.*

'You'll need to speak with Lieutenant Cummins.'

'Chief Showalter knows who I am. How about I talk to him?'

'He's in a meeting.'

Cummins had to have played basketball in middle school and high school. He was a minimum of six foot five and just the right kind of gangly. Even if he'd tripped all over himself and never managed to get the ball in that nasty little hoop, he was so stereotypically a starting center the coach had to play him, though the bald pate and the fringe of white hair would have kept him on the bench these days.

Cummins was no help, either. 'You need to be his lawyer.'

'His lawyer is en route from Chicago.'

'Well, I guess the Bradshaws have got the money.'

'What the hell's that supposed to mean?'

I'd irritated him. 'It's supposed to mean that the Bradshaws have the kind of money that can bring in Chicago lawyers. I'm sorry if I offended your delicate sensibilities.'

The woman at the desk snorted.

'His folks have already been here,' Cummins said. 'They were very nice people. They spent forty-five minutes with him and then left. The lawyer they mentioned was Kostik, from right here. Guess there's been a change of plans, huh?'

I would have to contact them. In the rush of things I'd forgotten to touch base. A very bad oversight.

'Listen, Lieutenant Cummins. I apologize for snapping at you.'

'All right.'

'But could you do me a favor?'

He glanced at the woman behind the desk, as if she was in charge. 'If I can.'

'Could you get a message to Chief Showalter?'

'He's with the city manager right now.'

'Could you tell him that Dev Conrad would appreciate just fifteen minutes alone with Cory Tucker?'

Again, the eye contact with the woman.

Then, 'I guess I could give it a shot.'

Tucker was in orange jail clothes and handcuffs.

Showalter hadn't sent him to County yet. Cummins had explained that they had eight cells on the second floor left over from the old jail.

Fear, confusion and defeat were all visible in the college boy's face as he thanked the blue-uniformed officer who seated him in the wooden chair at the wooden table on the opposite side of me.

The room was painted institutional green. Cigarette smoke from the old days still tainted the air.

'Fifteen minutes.' Not harsh, not friendly. She closed the door quietly.

He bowed his head. His wrists twisted against the cuffs. A curse was lost in his throat. He looked up. His dismay was palpable. 'What'll happen to me, Dev? This whole thing is insane. Showalter didn't even ask if I was guilty. He just assumed I was.'

'Standard stuff. Just trying to scare you. Jess and everybody else knows you had nothing to do with this.'

'I figured you'd all know better. At least, I hoped you would.'

'Think you can answer a few questions?'

'I'm pretty scattered right now. It doesn't feel real. But I'll try and answer what I can.'

'Thanks, Cory. The first thing I need to know is what they're telling you.'

'Telling me?'

'Why they charged you?'

'They found a rifle in my trunk. They seem to be sure it was the rifle somebody fired at the congresswoman.'

I had to play cop. Show no emotion. The setup was clear. Rage was my first and foremost feeling. Such a cheap, bullshit trick had been played on Cory. But for now it was working.

'How often do you look in your trunk?'

'Never. Unless I need to, I mean.'

'Do you remember where you went yesterday?'

'I worked for the campaign, mostly, except for an hour and a half when I worked the phones. One of the women got sick so I volunteered. I figured it'd be a good experience for me. I could include it on my résumé.' Bitter smile. 'Résumé. Like that matters right now.'

'How about last night? Where did you go?'

'A party at a friend's house.'

'Were there a lot of people there?'

'Yes. I had to park – that's it.'

'What's "it?"'

'There were so many people there I had to park almost a block away.'

'Is it a well-lit neighborhood?'

'No. It's kind of a slum. Fraternities rent it together and then have their parties down there. I'm not in a frat but some of my friends are so they invited me. That sounds like a good time to do it, doesn't it?'

'Perfect time. Somebody follows you around until they see an opportunity to slip the rifle in your trunk. How long were you at the party?'

'A few hours. The girl I was hoping to see there didn't show up so I went home early.'

'Straight home?'

'Yes.' Then, 'You should see my folks.' Now came the tears. He was a good kid who loved his folks. He had no trouble empathizing with how frightening this would be for them. And embarrassing. He fought crying. The tears just shimmered on the blue eyes.

'We've hired the best defense lawyer in Chicago.'

'But my folks said the bond was half a million dollars. Who am I, Jeffrey Dahmer? My folks don't have that kind of money and I sure don't want them to mortgage the house or anything.'

'The bond's being handled.' I was just working my way through my daily allotment of tall tales.

'It is?' I heard the first note of hope in his voice.

'The Bradshaw family is putting up the money.'

Or they would, as soon as I leaned on them.

'So I can get out of here?'

'Five hours max, I'd say.'

He forced back the tears. Grateful tears this time. Then he fell into reverie. 'I'm not perfect – I mean, I've shoplifted stuff in my life and I've done drugs I shouldn't have, but that was all in high school. Something like this . . . My mind wouldn't even *work* this way. I've never fired a gun in my life. I wouldn't know *how* to.' Then, directly to me, 'Do you think the whole thing was staged?'

'I'm not sure yet.'

'You were an investigator. Are you getting involved?'

'Yes, I am. Of course.'

'This'll cost her the election. That's the other thing. I can't believe it. She did so well with the debate and all—' Then, 'Sorry, I'm being such a baby about this.'

'You're hardly being a baby. You've been charged with a major felony.'

'Have you ever been arrested?'

'Three times. And once I thought they were going to put me away for a long, long time.'

'How did you get out of it?'

'I hired the best private investigator I could. An old friend from my army days. He proved I'd been set up. That I hadn't broken into our opponent's private office and crippled his security guard in the process.'

'But it was close?'

'Close enough that I had to consider the fact that I was going to spend seven to ten years in prison.'

'God.'

A tale nicely told. I was using up my allotment faster than usual.

And the tale had relaxed him, as I'd hoped it would. Carried him out of this smudgy little room and into the sunny autumn air where hardworking college kids like him should be.

Then the knock. The blue uniform. The voice neither harsh nor friendly.

'Man, I feel so much better talking to you, Dev. Thanks so much.'

'I'll see you soon.'

'You really think five hours max?'

'Five hours max.'

This one wasn't a lie. I believed he could be set free in five hours. Of course, if he wasn't he'd see it as a lie.

He thanked her again as she stood aside to let him walk through the door.

It was unlikely she was used to this kind of politeness.

TWENTY-THREE

Mike Edelstein was one of those Big Ten college fullbacks who'd managed to keep in shape both physically and mentally. He was as fierce in the courtroom as he'd been in his glory days at Michigan State.

For once he wore his suit coat as well as his suit pants. Blue pinstripes today. Except in the courtroom, he rarely wore the jackets. At parties you'd see him get rid of it within ten minutes of crossing the threshold. He reminded me of Lou Grant on the old *Mary Tyler Moore Show*. As he walked in, he said, 'I finally found another judge who might have one of those little jerk-off machines under his robes.'

Mike, like most of us, had loved the absolutely true story of the

Southern judge who managed to masturbate while his court was in session. The problem was two-fold: the machine made a faint whirring noise, and occasionally the judge started getting glassy-eyed and a little out of breath. Not only did a witness catch on to this, so did the cop who stood on the right side of the bench. His interpretation – a generous man – was that the judge was having medical problems. He was in his seventies. The witness, not generous at all, talked to a reporter about it and she suggested flat out that the old guy in the robes was somehow getting his rocks off. Intrepid reporter starts looking online for whack-off machines and finds the one, as it turned out, His Honor was using. His Honor was soon busted and relieved of his duties.

'Judge Flannagan. Kind of a young guy, too. But I keep hearing this very small noise – maybe a whirring noise. And every once in a while his head rolls back and I swear to God he starts breathing hard and sweating. What's that sound like to you?'

Then, before I could answer, 'Pretty crazy shit, huh? Those little machines.'

'You thinking of getting one?'

'I'd need a big one, my friend. A very big one.'

'A hotshot lawyer and modest, too. So what the hell are you going to do for Jess?'

He sat in one of the client chairs in my office. This was less than five hours after I'd called him. One of his clients had a private jet. Since Mike had saved him from doing a thirty-to-life sentence, he was a most generous benefactor.

'I wish it was a slam dunk for the Tucker kid,' Mike said. 'He's obviously been set up – unless he did it, of course – but that may not be easy to prove.'

'You say things like that just so you can charge more, don't you?'

The big bear smile. 'You're not half as dumb as you look.'

'Hard to believe that Cory would buy a rifle. He's pretty anti-gun. That part of Showalter's story doesn't work at all.'

'I'm working on that angle. But I can hear Showalter's version. Here you have a young man who's anti-gun, who tells me he's never even fired a gun of any kind before and you think that would be good for our case but, when you think about it, it can be argued very well the other way. He gets his hands on this rifle in some as yet undetermined way and does enough reading and enough practicing to know how to handle the rifle – he doesn't need to be a marksman. Jess isn't going to be shot, anyway. All he has to do is fire a few wild shots at her and it's mission accomplished.'

'So now Showalter will say that Jess was behind this directly? This wasn't just some staffer acting on his or her own?'

'That's where this is heading, Dev. And if you've heard the news in the last half hour, so is the press.'

As yet, Edelstein didn't know any of the background about Cindy or Grimes or the anti-government group. I spent the next fifteen minutes going through what I knew.

'We need to get Grimes on tape.'

'Easier said than done. But I'll give it a try.'

'How about Cindy? Can we get her on tape?'

'I'm pretty sure we can. But she's really scared.'

'I don't blame her.'

The door was closed. Impossible as it seemed, Abby's hand had a distinctive sound – knuckles against wood.

'Come in.'

Abby appeared.

'You remember Abby, Mike.'

'Of course. Hi, Abby.'

'Hi, Mike.'

'Abby, we're going over everything we know up to date. How about sitting in with us for a while? You live here and know the ground a lot better than we do.'

'And you're a hell of a lot better looking than Dev, too.'

'You sure he's your friend, Dev?'

'Yeah. If I pay him enough.'

Abby took a seat and it was back to work.

TWENTY-FOUR

Grimes didn't answer his front door. He didn't answer his side door. He didn't answer his back door, either.

But his Ford was parked at the curb, which meant he was probably inside unless Cindy had taken him somewhere.

The back door was locked but the large window opening on the kitchen was not. A bad oversight for somebody as paranoid as Grimes.

I climbed through it, the dusty sheer curtains almost making me sneeze as they rubbed against my face. I remembered my first day of training for being an army investigator. The brisk colonel teaching the course said that when trying to sneak into a building of any kind, try not to sneeze. It sounded reasonable at the time and it still sounded reasonable.

The appliances were a couple of decades old. The refrigerator made so much noise it probably kept the neighbors awake at night. A week's worth of dirty dishes was piled in the sink. A linoleum floor was scuffed into oblivion. A clock radio sat on the counter, along with a spice rack. A calendar with a sweet painting of Jesus on it hung from a tiny nail on one of the ancient wooden cupboards. The year was 2001. I wondered if his wife had hung it there. It was hard to imagine Grimes doing it.

The place smelled of the dirty dishes, beer and cigarette smoke.

I was just starting to move into the front of the house when Grimes appeared, pointing one of those old Savage carbines my dad and uncle used to carry when they went out and had a good time blasting away at deer, something they could never convince me to do.

'What the hell do *you* want?'

'You lied to me last night. You know who came to see you. He wanted the recorder. He thought you had it.'

'You better not say anything like that to poor Cindy. She's out of her mind already. Dave, he told me about the recorder the night the Bradshaw woman got shot at. Told me how scared he was. He said he just wanted out of his little group. Said he made the recording for his own protection. I thought of goin' to the police but I knew if I did he'd be in trouble.' Right there before me he went from tired to wasted. 'He didn't say so, but he likes to hide shit. He's like a little kid. He tells me about stuff he's got hidden but he never tells me where it is. But I got a pretty good idea.'

'Yeah?'

'He's got this trailer. I bet if you went through it carefully you'd be surprised what you'd find.'

I explained that I'd been out there but hadn't gone through the place thoroughly. 'Go back, then. Look it over real carefully.' Then, 'Shit. I need t'sit down.'

I followed him into the living room. He set the Savage down carefully on the couch and sat next to it. I took the armchair where you could sink to the vanishing point.

'All I give a damn about is Cindy.'

'I know that.'

'Dave's a good kid except he got mixed up with that group. All that crazy crap they talk. Revolution and all that. They're just the other side of what those hippies were like. Afghanistan was what fucked him up.'

'I'm sorry, Grimes. But now I want to hide Cindy somewhere.'

'I already arranged that. She's at this old friend of hers.'

'I'd like the phone number.'

He made the kind of sounds lungers make.

'I told her to stay away from the cops. I made her promise. I told her that if she loved me she wouldn't go to the police.'

He was right. Why the hell not? All over the western United States there were law enforcement officers signing on to anti-government groups. But no section of the country was exempt from the hysteria these people generated. Why not the Midwest?

'That's why they want the recorder. Dave probably named the cops in the group.'

'The son of a bitch who busted me up, I'd like a crack at him.'

'You should hide out someplace else, too, until this is over.'

'If the cops're involved in this, when do you think it'll be over? They won't rest till they get that recorder. And by the way, I ain't goin' anywhere. This is *my* place. I worked half my life payin' for it and I ain't about to run away.'

He was right. He wasn't running anywhere. He wouldn't even be *walking* anywhere. His years and his life had all caught up with him. Only one thing mattered to him now and that was Cindy's safety. But the responsibility of that had completely depleted him. He still had it in him to give out with raspy curses but there wasn't jack shit he could do about defending himself, let alone Cindy.

He yawned and then his head teetered to the right side of his shoulder. Just yesterday he'd been strong enough and tough enough to run away to his car when his two friends from the Skylight had

confronted me. Now he could barely stay awake. He needed to go
back to bed. I kept thinking of his heart problems.

'Where's your bedroom?'

He yawned again. 'Why?'

'You need to go back to bed.'

'Why?'

'Why? Because you can barely stay awake. This whole thing has
worn you out.'

'The hell it has.'

'I'm sick of arguing with you, Grimes. You need to sleep. Cindy's
as worried about you as you are about her.'

'Yeah?'

'Yeah.'

'She say that?'

'She didn't *have* to say that, you grumpy old bastard. Haven't
you ever seen the way she looks at you?'

The unthinkable. Tears in his eyes.

'Nothin's been the same since my wife died.'

'I'm sorry, Grimes. You're through until you get some sleep.'

Again his head teetered to the right. 'Yeah, I guess maybe I am.'

I got up, walked over to him and held out my hand.

'I'm going to help you get to bed.'

But even with tears in his eyes he was belligerent. 'I don't need
no help.'

'Right. So stand up then.'

'What?'

'Stand up.'

'Just get the hell out of here, you son of a bitch. This is my place
and nobody gives me orders in my place. Now go.'

His irascibility made him suddenly sound much stronger than he
was.

'You won't stand up because you're too weak to.'

'Weak? The hell I'm weak.'

And with that he did his angry best to show me that he was too
strong and too proud to accept any help from somebody like me.
He put a hand on the arm of the couch and began the process of
pushing himself to his feet. He almost fell over.

I grabbed his right arm, holding him up.

'Now,' I said, 'where the hell's your bedroom, Grimes?'

TWENTY-FIVE

The ride out to Dave Fletcher's Airstream was pleasant. I was heading there again because of what Frank Grimes had said about Dave Fletcher's habit of hiding things. This time I'd search the place.

It was another elegant autumn day.

As I left the car and approached the trailer I had a feeling of isolation; maybe it was the crows and the sudden and utter silence in this small valley. Not even the fall colors of the trees were quite as bright here. I had a schoolboy memory: the land around the House of Usher. Poe's sense of desolation.

I was within a few feet of the Airstream's door when I noticed the car oil on the grass. Its shine revealed its freshness. There wasn't much of it. I bent down and touched a fingertip to it. It was fresh as hell.

When I struck the trailer door with my hand it eased open.

There was a stench which was familiar to me. It was a terrible stench; the worst stench of all.

So when I went in and saw what was on the floor there was no surprise.

My guess was that the man I assumed to be Dave Fletcher had been dead for some time. He had been a short, thin man with a finely boned face. It was already discoloring. The stench made me tear up. I examined him at a glance. He'd been wearing a yellow shirt, so the two bullet wounds in his chest were easy to see.

I got out of there as quickly as I could. I walked ten feet from the Airstream and started taking in deep, clean breaths.

Then it was time to call Showalter on my cell phone.

For the local press, the recent days' events were definitely better than sex, except maybe for the kind that involves animals. To their satisfaction, a congresswoman had been brought down and now the body of a man had been found in mysterious circumstances.

Showalter dispatched six officers to commit due diligence on the crime scene. He then spent fifteen minutes in the trailer after telling me not to head back to town until he was finished talking to me.

I walked over to the wooded area and used my cell phone to call Cindy Fletcher. When she answered she said hello and then said, 'Your voice. Oh, God, I'm afraid I know what you're going to say. Dave's dead, isn't he?'

'I'm afraid he is, Cindy.'

'Where? How?'

I told her everything I knew.

She surprised me – and probably herself – by staying emotionless. 'He said they were going to kill him.'

'He said who was going to kill him?'

'He didn't say. He could get pretty dramatic sometimes so I didn't take him seriously, I guess. That's why I didn't tell you. Now I'm sorry I didn't.'

Then, 'He could be very trusting sometimes. Like a little kid. He told one of the cops that he'd made that recording. But afterward he realized that maybe this cop could have told someone in Showalter's little group about it. He could be such a little boy.'

I didn't try to stop her. She needed to weep and she wept. I just waited her out. She didn't recover so much as simply wear out.

'So they found him. That's what happened. They wanted that recorder. They found him and they killed him. That damned trailer. Neither of us went out there very often. There are snakes and rats from the river on the west side of it and you never knew who might come along at night. Dave always brought a rifle and a couple of handguns but I still didn't feel safe. I'm not sure he did either.'

I saw Showalter walking in my direction so I said a quick goodbye. No amenities.

'So how did you know Dave Fletcher?' Showalter said.

'I didn't know Dave Fletcher.'

Wind soughed in the pines and brought the scent to me as a gift. I needed something to comfort me. The events of the day had sapped my strength and my sense.

'Just out for a drive and you ended up back here?'

'I got a phone tip.' Lies come so easily to me.

'And, of course, you're going to tell me who called you.'

'I wish I could. Anonymous, of course.'

'They'd call you instead of the police.'

'I wish they'd called you instead of me. But what could I do?'

'You could have called me *before* you came out here.'

'How did I know it wasn't a crank call? I'm in the news because of Congresswoman Bradshaw. It could have been one of Dorsey's people just trying to run me around in circles.'

'Like you're trying to run *me* around in circles right now, huh?'

He had a good scowl. If he'd been an emperor he would have used it when he was thumbs-downing a fighter in the Coliseum. 'I hope you realize that I don't believe one fucking word you just said.'

'I'm sorry about that.'

'Sure you are.'

That old self-control I usually rely on couldn't be relied on this time. 'If you can't see that fucking rifle in Cory's trunk was a plant, then I wonder whose side you're on.'

He took two steps toward me. His face was as red as a drunk's on his birthday. 'What the hell are you saying?'

'I'm saying you owed the congresswoman a phone call before your press conference. I'm saying you shouldn't have been so quick to rule out a setup. And I'm saying the Dorsey folks are the ones who benefit.'

But then *his* self-control kicked in.

'It's going to be a pleasure nailing your ass to the wall, Conrad.'

I was getting the impression he didn't care for me all that much. I was also getting the impression – because he refused to even consider that Cory had been framed – that maybe he was involved in the police group himself.

As soon as I got in my car I called Cindy again. We needed to get our lies straight.

Grief had now become dazed withdrawal. She was playing hide-and-seek with herself. I repeated the lies three times then hung up with no reassurance that she would remember a single damned one of them.

TWENTY-SIX

When I got back to my office I learned two things quickly: Cory Tucker had been released on bond and Dorsey was demanding an 'immediate and thorough investigation' into whether Jess's 'attempted assassination' was a hoax or not. 'Hoax' was a loaded word.

I watched the replay of Dorsey's rant on my Mac. No TV huckster could have done any better. His last line was, 'Should she be headed back to Washington or headed to federal prison?'

Her crime wouldn't have been federal, but it sounded more ominous to slip the 'federal' in there.

Abby came in with a Starbucks (latte, I assumed) in one hand and a sheet of paper in the other.

'You know that governor of ours who should be in prison but isn't?'

Our esteemed governor – a fine representative of the opposition party – was being investigated for accepting bribes and helping condemn land that he and his close friends wanted to buy cheap as the basis for building an ultra-exclusive 'village.'

She held the paper out and let it flutter to my desk.

After reading it, I said, 'It's got to be fun for him to accuse other people of committing felonies.'

'He groped a friend of mine when we were in college.'

'Governor Anal Retentive?'

'He was dean of students then. After a football game we all ended up in this van going to a dinner at the president's house. Shelly and I were on the student council so the president asked us to attend. Anyway, the van got overcrowded and Shelly had to sit on his lap. We only had to go about five or six blocks but he managed to cop several cheap feels.'

'Why didn't she say something?'

'She wanted to but he could help her get financial aid for grad school.'

I grabbed my phone on the second ring. 'You need to get out here.' It was Ted.

'Why is that?'

'My dear wife has written something I think you should read before she presses "Send."'

'And what would that be, Ted?'

'Her resignation. Can you believe it? She wants to resign.'

Katherine opened the door.

'This is really bad, Dev. She really wants to resign.'

Emerald-green sweater, slimline jeans, Western boots. The attire of the fashionable coed. But a burned-out coed. The face was lined and the eyes dulled with exhaustion.

Nan walked up behind her and put her hands on Katherine's shoulders. Between Joel and Nan, Katherine did have a pair of caring parents after all.

'I thought you were going back upstairs for a nap.'

'I'm too worried about Mom,' Katherine said over her shoulder.

'Well, you obviously didn't sleep much last night so you need to at least lie down for a while. You look terrible, honey.'

Katherine put her hand over Nan's. 'She's always flattering me like this, Dev.'

But with little-girl obedience, Katherine said goodbye to me, turned around and walked slowly over to the grand staircase to begin her ascent to her room upstairs.

'I'll be so damned glad when this is all over. This whole house has lost its mind. Everybody snapping at each other and Ted calling up people and screaming at them. You sure can't count on him in a crisis.' If her own sweater and jeans didn't make her look like a coed, they certainly helped present her as an appealing middle-aged woman.

'How serious is Jess about resigning?'

'Serious, I think. I've begged her to stop watching TV and reading the news on her computer but she's fixated. And none of it's any good. The names they call her and the things they say about her.'

'You sound as if you've been spending time on your own computer.'

'I check it out every few hours but I don't stay on long. I keep hoping to see people in her own party come to her defense. But since none of them are sure if the shooting thing is true or not, they won't speak up. I think that hurts her more than anything.'

'I don't blame her. She has made a lot of supposed friends in Congress.'

'"Supposed" is right. Well, come on. I may as well take you to her little office. I don't think you've ever seen it, have you?'

'You're right, I haven't. We usually meet in the living room or Ted's den.'

'It's quite the place.'

Three steps into Jess's office, I realized that Nan had been trying to prepare me for a time machine of Jess's political career from her days as a college volunteer through her four terms as a state legislator to her two terms as a congresswoman. I'd always known that Jess had the true pol's lust for being elected. But seeing an office that was a shrine of framed photographs, campaign posters, pennants, bumper stickers, newspaper editorials and so much more, I realized how much she was her career. Before any other role she may have fulfilled, her political role was the defining one.

And the same for Ted. There he was in half the photos. This was what united them. This career that they both fed; this political career that they both spent night and day nurturing and sustaining.

The largest photograph was of the two of them in evening clothes dancing through the night at some Washington ball. They were the center of attention, the floor to themselves as others in evening clothes stood aside watching and applauding them. How dreamlike that moment must have been for them. In this most exalted and important of cities, to be feted this way.

I went to the window and looked out at the rolling landscape of their estate. A man in a white T-shirt, jeans and a straw hat was astride a green John Deere riding mower. But the real show was a hawk soaring above the pine windbreak. For all their hunting ferocity there was a fragility in their flight that made them seem vulnerable. But I had to smile at my naiveté. I doubted that hawks seemed vulnerable in any way to their prey, which included pets as familiar as small dogs and puppies, small cats and kittens, plus rabbits and guinea pigs.

I glanced at the rest of the photographs. Joel standing with a heavyset young man, holding a rake. The man had an Old Testament beard. And there was a lone photo of Katherine when she was probably ten.

Then Jess was there. A Northwestern sweatshirt and slacks. And a lighted cigarette.

'I see somebody called you.'

'Do me a favor. Let's just get rid of this resignation bullshit, all right?'

'It's not bullshit to me.'

'I'm sure you realize that if you resign you're admitting guilt.'

'Right now I couldn't care less. Believe it or not, Dev, I have some dignity left. The things they're saying not just about me but also Ted—'

She went over and sat down in front of her Mac. The lid was down.

'The election's already over anyway. So what's the point? Why not resign?'

'Look around, Jess. You've built this grotto to you and Ted. This is your life here. Your entire life.' I wanted to point out that she didn't even have a photo of her daughter on the walls. 'So you're going to walk away from it all because you got set up?'

'Yes, I got set up and nobody's done a damned thing about it. Including you.'

'I'm working on it as hard as I can. There are things I haven't told you yet.'

'Unless those things include the name of the person responsible for setting us up, I don't want to hear them. Poor Ted is half insane.'

He'd cheated on her. He'd stolen her spotlight from time to time. And he'd even given her some of the worst political advice ever uttered by a so-called 'expert.' But none of this mattered because they were symbiotic.

'You may as well go, Dev. I've made up my mind.'

'What's Ted saying about all this?'

'He's like you. He's begging me to change my mind. He keeps thinking if he reminds me long enough about all the big parties people have in the winter months that I'll weaken. But I won't. There's a time to fight and a time to retreat.'

'Did you just make that up? He's worried about the fucking parties?'

'Wow. The f-word.'

'Do me one favor then, Jess.'

'Whenever you ask me that it's always something I don't want to do so I don't know why you even bother asking.'

'Just give it another forty-eight hours.'

'No.'

'This is one of the biggest decisions of your life.'

'*The* biggest.'

'See. You even agree with me. So what the hell difference will it make if you give it forty-eight more hours?'

'No.'

'Twenty-four.'

'That's too much like a bad movie. "I'm giving you twenty-four hours."'

'Jess, c'mon. Get serious here.'

'I am "serious here," in case you haven't figured that out by now.'

'Twenty-four hours.'

'I suppose I can do that. But don't call me unless you have somebody to arrest. And please get out of here now, because you are really pissing me off. You of all people I expect to be my friend and understand why I've made this decision.'

I was tempted to touch her in some way. Just a small human sense of contact, of caring. But I knew better.

'That's what I'm trying to be, Jess.' I spoke as quietly as I could. 'Your friend.'

But then she was crying. And I was leaving.

TWENTY-SEVEN

J ust before I slid the card that unlocked the door of my hotel room into the slot I heard a faint sound from inside. Or was it from inside? Though the hotel was new and well constructed, sounds still carried occasionally. Maybe what I heard was from one of the adjoining rooms.

But in case it had come from my room I stopped and put my ear to the door. I heard all those ghost noises from the giant entity that ran the place. Electricity, plumbing, the inner structure itself. Ghost whispers, but audible if you listened for a minute or so.

Ghost whispers but nothing more.

I wished I'd listened longer or listened more competently, because as soon as I stepped inside I faced the same pretty brunette I'd met at Jess's and who had later followed me. Karen Foster.

She was wearing a fashionable gray business suit with a notched lapel and single button holding it together. The matching pants were flared slightly above gray leather two-inch heels. The small black-framed eyeglasses only enhanced the appeal of her dark eyes.

As a fashion accessory her right hand held a Glock. She kept it pointed directly at my chest. 'Why don't you close the door and come in?'

'Very nice. I assume you have a search warrant.'

'No, but I can get one in a few minutes if I need one.'

'Retroactive search warrants. That's quite a concept.'

She stood close to the end table next to the near end of the couch and carefully placed the Glock on the table.

'Why don't you sit down so we can talk?'

What the hell. Between her looks and her manner I was willing to be charmed.

I sat on the couch and she sat in the chair at the small table next to the window.

'I don't think Cory Tucker had anything to do with the so-called shooting the other night.'

'Good for the first part. He didn't. Not so good for the second part. The "so-called" shooting. We don't know that yet.'

'I'm on your side, so you don't have to keep up the public-relations thing. The shooting was a fake and you know it.'

'I'm willing to consider it, I guess.'

She nodded. 'I want to help you find out who set Cory Tucker up.'

'Why would you want to help me?'

'I'll tell you some other time.'

'Why not now?'

She eased back in her chair and smiled at me. She wasn't going to explain.

'Maybe Grimes can help both of us.'

'How do you know about Grimes?'

'You led me to him.'

'I knew you followed me to the Airstream but I didn't realize you were following me before that.'

'I changed cars a lot. And if I say so myself, I'm a very good tail.' Then, 'I got interested in you the night of the fake shooting. I knew right away that the whole thing was staged – I think a lot of people did. I assumed that since you were the congresswoman's campaign manager you were in on it. I even thought that maybe you were behind it all. The sympathy vote. Poor little congresswoman and some big, bad assassin. So I started following you. I know about Grimes and his granddaughter, Cindy. I know that you've spent some time with them, that is. Unfortunately, I didn't have Grimes's house bugged, so I have to ask you what all three of you talked about.'

'I may tell you later on.'

'You're sort of a bastard, aren't you?'

I needed a cup of coffee and so, it turned out, did she.

There was sufficient in the coffeepot so I popped two cups in the microwave and brought one of them back to her.

'This could all be a trap.'

'Of course it could. Showalter could have sent me here to pretend I wanted to help you so you'd tell me everything you know and I'd run back and tell him.'

'Showalter? If you're going to help me that means you're not going to help him.'

'Let's just say I don't think much of him. I'll tell you why some other time.'

I pretended to enjoy my coffee more than I did. I was trying to puzzle through this pitch she was giving me. She could be an exquisite liar. So good that she was able to make me think that she had some profound hatred for Showalter – just hinting at it, wisely not putting it into words – and thus making me believe her story absolutely.

I thought of a way to test her. 'Showalter said he got a phone call tipping him to the fact that the rifle was in Cory's trunk. You have any way of checking if there was such a call?'

'The desk person that night might know.'

'Would you check on that?'

'My Girl Scout leader used to do stuff like this.'

'Like what?'

'Give us little tests to see if we were loyal to her. There was this other girl's mom who wanted to be the leader. So we got all these loyalty tests.'

'That was pretty heavy stuff for little girls.'

'Prepared us for the real world. So I don't mind.'

'You're pretty good.'

'I'm better than "pretty good."'

'I'll bet you are.' Then, 'You've been here longer than I have. Don't you think it's possible that they set this up knowing that it would look as if Jess and I did it and that it would backfire on us? And isn't Dorsey likely behind it one way or another?'

'Maybe.'

'That's all you've got? "Maybe."'

'I said maybe because I just don't know. Not yet.' Then, 'Very good coffee, thank you. But now I need to go. I have another appointment.'

'Wow. That's kind of abrupt.'

'Not much I can do about it. I really do have an appointment.'

I walked her to the door. The warmth of her body and the scent of her perfume dragooned me into saying, 'We could always continue this at dinner. That way you could answer my question about why you want to take Showalter down.'

She wasn't inclined to change her mind and explain herself. The dark eyes held mine for a long, pleasant moment. 'How about the main dining room downstairs at seven or so?'

'Sounds great.'

'Are you a little bit afraid of me?'

'Yes.'

'Good. Because I'm a little bit afraid of you.'

PART THREE

TWENTY-EIGHT

'd planned to catch up on my other races in my room but I was too distracted by the idea of working with Karen Foster to concentrate, so I headed back to the office.

'Katherine's in your office,' Donna said. 'I told her it would be all right for her to wait for you in there.'

'Of course.'

In her amber blouse and brown skirt, her blonde hair done in a shining ponytail, Katherine resembled her mother more than usual. It was an elegant look, without quite being disdainful. For once the melancholy in her usual gaze had been replaced with something walking right up to the edge of happiness.

'I think I've come up with a really good idea, Dev.'

'I'm sure you have. You have a lot of good ideas.'

'I know you're just saying that because you're such a nice guy, but I'm serious.'

'So am I. So tell me your idea.'

'That we hold a support rally for my mom tomorrow night. A huge one. If we put everyone to work on it I think we can make it impressive.'

'Now that's a good idea.'

'Seriously?'

'Yes. I want to get your mother out of her "resignation" mood.'

'I don't think she's really serious about that. She's a lot more serious about the divorce, I'm afraid.'

Katherine was giving me news that could make the campaign even more difficult. I tried not to pound my fist on the desk and start running around screaming.

A divorce?

'I guess you hadn't heard about it. The second I said it I regretted it. The look on your face.'

'When did this start?'

She was talking past the hurt. The eyes were mournful once again but the voice remained purposeful. She was a grownup now. She knew how to fake it.

'You know Dad has a new one.'

'So I hear. I thought their marriage counselor had set them up pretty well.'

'For almost two years. But then he met this intern at his lawyer's office.'

'Intern? How old is she?'

'Twenty-three. She looks like Audrey Hepburn.'

'Good for her.'

A deep breath. 'Mom is convinced this one is for real.'

'She didn't think that about the other ones.'

'No. I would never have put up with it, but she did. She even had a small fling herself once – she never told me who with – but she felt guilty about it. Even if Dad wasn't faithful, she wanted to be. She just waited him out. And it always worked out well. He got tired of them. Mom even had it figured out mathematically. Fourteen weeks tops.'

'Wow.'

'She started telling me all this when I was fifteen. I hated him for it but I had to admit in a painful way it was sort of fascinating. Fourteen weeks. She'd tell me when he had a new one – she trained me to see the signs. And hear them. The only time I ever heard my father sing was when he was having an affair. It was so stupid. You'd think he'd be aware of something like that.' A soft laugh. 'He has a really terrible voice. And he always sang the same song. "Lost in Love." The song is as bad as his voice. Really lame. Mom always wondered if he sang it to his girlfriends.'

'So does he know about the divorce?'

'Oh, yes. They scream about it every night. He doesn't want it to happen.'

'Has it occurred to him that he could give up Audrey baby?'

'He says she's not the point. He says it's just another one of his flings. He keeps saying they should go back to the marriage counselor but she says it's too late for that.'

'How do you feel about it?'

Another deep sigh. 'Crazy as it sounds, I don't want them to get divorced. I just want him to remember his age and to act it. He has this "star" thing about himself and it can really get embarrassing.'

The smile managed to be dismissive and fond at the same time. 'It's like him wearing that black turtleneck for the interview. I wouldn't have blamed that poor director if he'd shot my father.'

'I think that crossed his mind.'

'She won't do anything about it until after the election, of course. Whatever she says otherwise, she wants to go back to Washington and stay there till she's about a hundred and forty. You know she was so wealthy growing up that she didn't value things. She had it all. Holding office is the only thing that she's ever had to fight for.'

It was time to circle back. 'I'll get hold of Abby. She knows all the local people we'll need to set up this rally. I think I'll ask your mother if she'd agree to do a short live interview on the local news before the rally.'

'That could be pretty grim for her.'

'We need to fight back. We need to reassure the base that we haven't given up.' I'd automatically slipped into canned-speech land. But I needed to hear it myself. 'We know that Cory Tucker is innocent. We know that somebody set him up and set us up. We know that the press has taken Showalter's word for things without doing any serious investigating on their own.'

'You're right. I'll talk to her about it, too.'

Her cell phone played a Mozart piece. She slipped it out of her small brown leather purse and checked the screen. 'It's Mom.'

'You talk to her. I'll walk over to Abby's office and give her the heads-up.'

'What if Mom says no to the rally and the interview?'

'With you and me both working on her, what chance does she have?'

For just a moment, her smile redeemed all the woes of the world.

'I like the way you think, Dev.'

TWENTY-NINE

Karen Foster was cute, smart and late.

I finally asked to be seated because I wanted an isolated table and the tables were going quickly.

It was easy to tell that the main restaurant in the hotel had recently been redecorated. The faint odor of paint and sawn lumber was in the air in a few places. Dramatic black and red tables and chairs lent the place a boldness that took a while to get used to. The floor was equally dramatic with striking shafts of gray and red. The light sources were concealed in gleaming black boxes along the black linen-covered walls. I was either in an experimental art gallery or some kind of avant-garde spaceship. I wasn't sure which.

Abby called on my cell phone. I'd left her a message about organizing the TV interview and the rally.

'You don't want much, do you?'

'I really apologize. But I'm busy, too.'

'I'm only teasing you. The rally is easy. I just called Jean Fellows and she'll have the place packed with volunteers and their families. There's a bandstand we can use. And as far as the TV interview, all three stations'll want it. I'll pick the one that's been least hostile toward Jess.'

'That sounds reasonable.'

'I was hoping we'd do something like this. Ted told me that she will barely leave her office at home for food or bathroom privileges. He also said she won't talk to him much.'

She needed to be aware of everything that was going on.

'They're getting a divorce.'

'What? Where did you hear that?'

'Katherine. In my office a while ago.'

'Has Jess lost her mind? No wonder she won't speak to him.' Then, 'It's the new bimbo, isn't it?'

'Yeah.'

'But he's had so many in the past. What's so special about this one? I mean, he's *always* been a shitty husband. If they had a national competition for shitty husbands he'd be in the top three.'

'Jess thinks he's serious about this one.'

'He's serious about *all* of them.'

'Fourteen weeks. Jess worked out the math.'

'I wish he'd stick his dick in a light socket.'

'He may already have done that. But she'll wait till after the election.'

She paused before she said it. 'We're not going to win this one, are we?'

'O ye of little faith.'

'Whenever you get religious I know we're in trouble.'

I kept thinking of Katherine's sweet face; seeing it always tugged me back to my own daughter's face over the years. I was old enough now to realize that I would die knowing that I'd cheated her out of my time and attention. I'd chosen the road over her. There was no way back. The most sacred relationship I'd ever had and I'd violated it. There were no windows in here to see the gathering dusk but, even unseen, it worked on me. I wanted to use one of my lie allotments on myself, convince myself that now it didn't matter so much anymore because Sarah was about to be a new mother. But I knew better.

She came in quickly and captured many male gazes.

Tonight she presented herself in a becoming combination of blue blouse and gray skirt that fashionably favored her form. She also wore a look of anger.

A waiter tried to catch up with her but didn't succeed. She had seated herself before he reached the table. 'I haven't been able to lose him.'

She wanted Scotch and soda and I wanted a refill on my coffee.

'Who?' She was spoiling the pleasure of enjoying her pert good looks.

'Wade. The assistant chief of police.'

'He's following you?'

'Showalter must have put him on me after I left the station today. I thought I'd lost him about half an hour ago. I ran him around in circles but somehow he found me again. That's why I'm late – I was trying to lose him.'

'What makes Showalter so suspicious of you?'

Instead of answering, she said, 'There's Wade.'

I don't know what I expected, but whatever it was I didn't get it. I must have assumed he was going to be the Showalter Marine type. Instead he was a pleasant-looking man in an inexpensive blue suit. He looked somewhat uncomfortable being in an upscale place like this.

'Don't let the next-door-neighbor act fool you, Dev.'

'What act?'

'Wade's act. The friendly, helpful type. He's the sharpest detective on the force and the best interrogator because he's so quiet and polite. I enjoy watching him work. It's like watching a great athlete.'

'You like him?'

'Let's say I understand him. His grandfather and his father were both police chiefs here. He was supposed to be next. But the city council got all hot on Showalter when he sent in his app. Looked macho in the Marine uniform. They wanted Clint Eastwood.'

'But Wade stayed on?'

'I don't know Wade that well – nobody does except his wife – but my sense of things is that he's just waiting for Showalter to screw up. Then the job'll be his.'

'But he's following you.'

'He's doing what Showalter tells him to. He's very careful to be respectful to Showalter. When the council does turn on Showalter – and three of the six who voted for him now have second thoughts – Wade doesn't want it to look as if he was anything but professional with Showalter.'

'But again, he's following you.'

She grinned with cute little white teeth. 'Nobody's perfect.'

When her Scotch came she drank half of it right off.

'I'm not really a drunk.' Then, 'I'm wondering if Showalter somehow found out who I really am. Maybe that's why Wade is following me.'

'Who you really are? I'm shocked you've been holding out on me.'

'Sure you are. And I'm shocked that you haven't admitted that we're both looking for the same recorder.'

'How do you know about the recorder?'

A little more Scotch.

'There are six of them in Showalter's little group. I put an electronic device on one of their cars. They tavern hop a lot. And talk a lot.' Then, 'There were only four of them in the group when Showalter was in Peoria several years ago. One of them was my stepbrother.'

'Now we're getting to why you hate Showalter.'

She shrugged her slender shoulders and stared at the hands she'd folded on the table.

'I don't blame Showalter for recruiting Denny into his little group of cops. Denny had always been a bad cop. Beating up people.

Ripping off drug dealers. He might even have tried a little blackmail.'

'I can't see why you liked him so much.'

'I didn't. But Showalter killed him and I promised my step-father that I'd prove it someday. My own father was a miserable drunk. He used to pound on my mother two or three times a month. He hit her so hard one time that she permanently lost hearing in one ear and later on he beat her again so badly that she now has a limp. We finally ran away one night – to a small town in Colorado – and he was never able to find us. Then my mom met a policeman, Don Sheridan, and married him. He was the finest man – finest person besides my mother – I've ever met. My real father was a surgeon so we never had the creature comforts he'd given us, but from the time I was eleven I considered Don my real father.

'I knew I needed to get into Showalter's police department, so I joined a force in Montana and worked there for three years. In addition to that, I'd gone to college back east for four years so I wasn't well known in the area anymore. I had a hacker help me create a different background for myself. It all worked out, even though it was a long shot. I just kept thinking of Don.

'He could have had a happy life with my mother except he was saddled with Denny. There was something missing in my stepbrother. I didn't learn until later on that it was called sociopathology. Whatever was good for Denny was good for the world. That's how he thought and lived. He was four years older than me and didn't like me at all. I think he was jealous of how much Don loved me. He could have turned that around. Don really loved him but Denny had broken his heart so many times by stealing from him, piling up his car and beating kids up. Denny scared me – his temper, I mean.

'Right out of high school, Denny went into the Marines. Don had hopes they'd turn Denny into the son he'd always wanted. But when he came out he was even worse. He had a real swagger then and his temper was probably twice as bad as it had been. We were living in Peoria then and that was how Denny met Showalter. Oh, I forgot to mention that Denny was a real racist when he got out of the service. He had connections to all these groups. He was always telling Don about them, trying to get him to go to some of these meetings, but Don never would. He wasn't like that.

'Showalter told Denny he wanted to build some kind of compound so three of them started robbing banks in other parts of the state.'

'Including Showalter?'

'Of course not. He wanted to give them the "privilege" of serving the cause by themselves. They raised a fair amount of money. That's where Showalter got involved. He "guarded" the money for them. It was a lie, of course. His whole thing with the racism and the compound was just a ruse to get them to collect money for him. They had close to three hundred thousand dollars when two of them got shot and killed during a robbery.'

'Was Denny along?'

'Yes. But he got away. Showalter said that they needed to lay low for a while. One day Denny asked him about the money and the compound. Denny was pretty sharp about most things but he hadn't figured out that Showalter was a con artist. Until that day. Showalter planted some of the robbery money in his apartment and then claimed that he'd confronted Denny about it and Denny had drawn his weapon. Showalter didn't have any choice but to kill him. That was the story he gave, anyway. It made the national news, then he got invited to this big police convention. I guess the speech he gave about dishonest cops was pretty good stuff. He even got interviewed on *60 Minutes*.'

'How did you learn about all this?'

'Denny told Don about it a few days before he was killed. Don said Denny didn't regret anything – not about the racist group or robbing banks, not even the bank teller who'd been shot pretty badly by one of the other men. He just wanted Don to know the truth. He said if he was killed it would be by Showalter. Don had to figure out some of it by himself after Denny died, but I'm sure he was right.'

'So what did Don do?'

'Went to the DA. But the DA said that given Denny's history and the fact that the only person making these claims was Denny's father . . .'

'Nothing?'

'Nothing.'

'You think Showalter's running the same scam here?'

'Maybe if we can ever find that recorder we'll know for sure. But my guess would be yes. Dave Fletcher was perfect for him. He wanted somebody to follow, to believe in. Showalter knows how to play the role. But he didn't bet on Dave making a recording.'

My eyes shifted to Wade across the way. He had been watching us then quickly looked away.

'Now do I get to know about Grimes?'

I smiled. 'Yeah, what the hell.'

I spent a few minutes bringing her up to date: how Cindy had called me, how Grimes had scoped me out and how he claimed at first that he'd suffered a head wound for no apparent reason. And then he'd told me more about Dave Fletcher and the recorder.

The food was good and we relaxed enough to talk about our lives. I probably told a few more stories about my daughter Sarah than I needed to and she probably told a few more tales about her twice-married and very glamorous sister, but I liked her and I sensed she liked me. And I was touched by her relationship with her step-father. Nailing Showalter was a holy quest for her; she managed not to sound deranged about it. The few people I'd known who were shaping their lives around vengeance had sometimes turned out to be as dangerous as the people they were chasing. But it was pretty difficult to argue with her. Not all dirty cops are menaces to the society they pretend to serve. They're dishonorable, but taking a few bucks here and there is just the kind of capitalism Wall Street practices. Unfortunately Showalter was the worst kind of cop and needed to be brought down.

'I'd like to talk to Grimes again. Want to come along?'

'What about my friend Wade over there? He'll follow me.'

'Yeah. But I know a way to shake him.'

Leaning on my army days again, I told her how my first boss, a colonel, had outlined a way to lose a tail. You needed yourself and a cohort to do it.

'Pretty slick, Dev. As long as Wade doesn't figure it out.'

'Worth a try.'

'You know something?' Karen said. 'I've really enjoyed this, thanks.'

THIRTY

The trick was simple enough.

As we were leaving the restaurant, we agreed on a meeting point, a pharmacy in a strip mall near the constituency office. I'd been in there once and knew that there was an alley behind it.

I got there a few minutes before she did and pulled up next to the back door of the place. It didn't take long. She came hurrying out the door and climbed into the car, leaving Wade sitting across the street from the front of the pharmacy, waiting for her.

Grimes's house was once again dark.

A full moon outlined it, doing it no favors.

Even bathed in gold the stark shambles were as ugly as ever. Urban gothic. His Ford was not out front.

We agreed that she'd knock on the front door while I walked around back.

The Ford wasn't parked on the narrow patch of gravel in back, either.

The neighborhood was quiet. No teenagers driving up and down. No music shaking the stars. No shouts from arguing couples. Her knocks were sharp as gunshots.

A tomcat on the grass behind me got all operatic for half a minute and the smell of an overflowing garbage can made me wince.

The back door was unlocked so it was at this point that I brought out my Glock. Grimes's religion was paranoia. There was no way he would have left the back door unlocked.

I walked to the front door and let Karen in. Even in the shadows I could see that her Glock was also drawn.

I remembered the American flag table lamp on the end table next to the couch.

I called out, 'Grimes? It's Dev Conrad.'

I started checking the house out room by room. None of them gave any indication that there had been trouble. No blood. Nothing knocked over or smashed.

Each room was a museum. The huge TV console with the ten-inch screen in the spare room. The record albums in the living room by Stevie Wonder and Derek and the Dominos and Fleetwood Mac. The closet with two tie-dyed shirts and a pair of red-and-blue-whirled bell bottoms.

The basement smelled from age and disrepair. The floor and the walls were wet and moisture had seeped into the stacks of magazines and newspapers that marked him as a hoarder of some kind.

When we got back upstairs the phone shrieked in the silence. I walked over to it and picked up.

'Who's this?'

'Dev Conrad, Cindy.'

'Oh – oh, God, Dev. I didn't recognize your voice and it scared me. How come Granddad didn't answer?'

'He's not here.'

She needed to prepare herself for what she said next. 'He has Dave's recorder. He told me that tonight on the phone. Dave gave it to him because he was scared to keep it himself. And this is how crazy he is now. He said he's going to sell it to Showalter. He said it's his turn to have some money.' Finally, she was able to say, shakily, 'I told him not to do it.'

'Showalter will kill him.'

'I told him the same thing. But he said he'd made a deal with them. They were going to pay him a hundred thousand dollars for it and once he got the cash he would tell them where to find it. He wouldn't listen to me. You know how stubborn he is.'

'I'll do my best to find him before it's too late, Cindy. I'll call you later.'

After I hung up, Karen said, 'I could hear pretty much everything. I could almost feel sorry for him. But greed's making him stupid.'

'Yeah,' I said, 'imagine that. Greed making somebody stupid.'

Then we got out of there.

THIRTY-ONE

'**B**e weird if somebody killed her *tonight*.'

I suppose at most other times he would have irritated, if not enraged me. A woman is shot at and you show up to see if maybe tonight the shooter will return and get lucky.

But most people there were thinking that. Most, being decent prairie people, were hoping that wouldn't be the case. They worried about it.

I couldn't judge this man's intentions for saying that. Certainly there were some at the rally who wouldn't have minded seeing it happen. They'd turned out to boo and ridicule her. They'd come to support Dorsey. Others just wanted some excitement, the kind you could talk about to your grandkids. *Oh, yes, kids, I was there the night that congresswoman got killed. Two shots. One in the head and one in the chest. Never forget anything like that no matter how old you get.*

So all I said was, 'Yeah, but the odds are against it.'

Something in my tone must have alerted him to my disapproval of what he'd said.

'Hey, I don't *want* to see it. I'm just saying.'

'I know, I know.'

He was a young husband – not even thirty, probably. Bears cap and sad start on a goatee, standing next to an even younger wife. Her holding the blue-blanketed infant, a four- or five-year-old girl clinging to him.

I nodded and moved away.

He'd had no idea who I was but we live in the land of paranoia. In the case that Jess actually *was* assassinated he'd probably feel guilty. And if he didn't, his wife would remind him of his words and then he'd be obliged to at least fake feeling guilty. When he'd spoken his wife had frowned and hugged her infant even tighter.

It was colder than I would have liked. I'd been hoping for five, six hundred people. We'd gotten four at most. Thirty-five degrees is a little chilly for many people.

The setting was a large city park with a bandstand. When Jess appeared that was where she'd be when she addressed the crowd.

I counted eighteen uniforms from three different groups. Local, state and a security firm Ted had personally hired. They split up, checking out the crowd, the wooded area and the area near the parking lot. A lean, mean man in a tan uniform and a heavy vest stood on the bandstand, carefully surveying the crowd and the wooded area to the left. Though the AK-47 was the weapon of choice these days, his was an M-16. A bit old-fashioned, but God help you if you ever caught a bullet from one.

There were fifteen minutes to go before Jess appeared.

A nice-looking young black TV reporter and her heavyset white cameraman knew who I was and trapped me between a wedge of crowd and the left side of the bandstand.

'Susan Harrison, Channel 4, Mr Conrad.'

I knew who *she* was. She'd been assigned to Jess since the staged shooting scenario had surfaced. She was one of those reporters who was a master at sounding friendly and accusatory at the same time. There's a special place in hell for these people.

With the camera rolling, she said, 'Everybody's asking if the congresswoman is nervous about coming here tonight. Who would know better than her campaign manager, Dev Conrad?'

'We're all a little on edge, Susan. I think that's only natural.'

'Some people say she has nothing to be nervous about if the shooting the other night was staged.'

'Well, some people think the earth is flat. That theory has yet to be proved.'

'One of your volunteers has been arrested for staging it.'

'He's been arrested but that doesn't mean he's done it.'

'Are you saying he's innocent?'

'Yes, that's what I'm saying.'

She couldn't keep the pleasure out of her appealing gaze. She'd gotten exactly the kind of sound bite that would play well at ten o'clock. She'd forced the campaign on the defensive. When you did that you always made the target sound guilty.

'Well, I join everybody here and at home, Mr Conrad, in hoping that there are no problems for the congresswoman tonight and that everything goes smoothly, whether the other night was staged or not.'

If I'd known where her car was I would have torched it.

For the past twenty minutes Abby had been working the crowd, trying to get them to volunteer for knocking on doors and working the phones at campaign headquarters. She wore a cheery red coat, cut quite fine, and looked damned appealing in it.

Now she stood next to me, the carnal scent of her perfume mixing with the silver of her breath.

'Well, if they actually come through, I got eight phone people and nine door knockers.'

'I'd say that's a very good night.'

'*If* they come through. That's always the problem.'

The brass band came from nowhere. Six older gents in heavy winter jackets and straw hats climbed the bandstand steps and played a Dixieland piece that cleaned your ears. The noise and the cold brought back memories of high-school football games on Friday nights. Ever the athlete, I sat in the stands and smoked Winstons. The music was welcome, giving the freezing crowd new energy.

I heard sudden noise behind me. A small caravan had pulled into the parking lot. Jess had arrived, escorted by three police cars with flashing red lights painting the surroundings.

The officers brought her to the bandstand in a formal way the other side would make fun of. She was lost inside six bear-sized police officers. They marched her to the bandstand and up the steps. The lean, mean sharpshooter with the M-16 managed to look even leaner and meaner.

A man was testing the stand-up microphone. It screeched a few times but the sound was mostly lost in the music of the brass band.

Jess waved and smiled. She wore a severely tailored dark blue coat. She always worried about looking too good – as did every campaign runner she'd ever had – so tonight she'd gone easy on the makeup. The face was a little wan and the dark lines under the eyes suggested concern. I wondered if they were real or if Ted had convinced his makeup person to put them on. Whichever, they were a nice touch.

Now both the band and the applause battled the air for dominance.

I saw the cheeks of women and a few men that glistened with tears.

I saw hands holding up the kind of lighted candles people use at rock concerts.

I saw a huge sign unfurl that read: JESS BRADSHAW FOR PRESIDENT!

She modestly waved for all the celebrating to stop. And then she began.

She did not play to the other night at first. She relied on a version of her stump speech. The issues we faced, the way she wanted to help lead the country, the terrible ways Dorsey wanted to change America. It was her version of a State of the Union address and like that increasingly hollow speech it was contrived for audience participation. Every fourth line got applause. The newsbites would show the genuine enthusiasm she inspired. Not that there weren't a few boos from a small group at the back. A new sign had appeared in their midst: WE WANT OUR COUNTRY BACK, BRADSHAW. At least they weren't waving any guns. Small mercies in this era of a Supreme Court bent on turning us into Beirut.

The sudden silence from Jess certainly got everybody's attention. She spent a few seconds shifting positions slightly, then turned her head so she could clear her throat.

'I'm sure you've been waiting for me to speak to the accusation that the shots fired at me the other night were part of some conspiracy to win this election. I think that those of you who've followed my time in the State House and later in the United States Congress trust me enough to know that I would never under any circumstances be part of anything so deceitful. I know I'm in a tough race – the toughest of my career as a public servant.'

The applause was loud enough to sway trees and crack windows.

But she waved it down. 'I really appreciate your support and faith in me. But this is difficult – painful – for me to talk about, so I'd really appreciate it if you'd just let me finish.'

She paused once again.

'One of my volunteers has been arrested for setting up the shooting. The police claim that they found the rifle in the trunk of his car. I don't know Cory Tucker well but the people in my campaign who do assure me that he's a very intelligent, honest, hardworking young man who'd never do anything like this.

'The important word in what I just said is "intelligent." If you were to fake a shooting like this you would have to be very stupid to think you'd get away with it. Law enforcement would see through it pretty quickly, and they have.'

These would be, as she'd told me when I suggested admitting that the assassination attempt had been, in fact, contrived, the most difficult words to speak. Wouldn't admitting that the incident had been a fraud simply sound like a confession?

'What I'm saying is that somebody did stage this assassination attempt and staged it in such a way that it would clearly be exposed as a fake – and then planted the rifle in Cory Tucker's trunk so it would appear that we concocted the whole thing ourselves.'

This time she did not try to stop the applause.

I knew how afraid she was now. I was anxious myself. Those who'd doubted us would cry that we'd come up with this pathetic spy-novel conspiracy story to save ourselves now that everybody knew we were liars. Dorsey would use Showalter to discredit Jess's words and I doubted that more than one or two on the task force would speak up on her behalf. But I'd also suggested one more thing to say.

'I'm asking the United States Justice Department to launch an investigation into this attempt to destroy not only my campaign but the life of a very decent young man who is now in great jeopardy.'

She didn't try to stanch the applause this time either. The boos and shouts were correspondingly louder as well.

Admitting that the assassination attempt had been staged and then calling for a federal investigation to be launched at least demonstrated to our admirers and our detractors that we were eager to fight back.

It was just then that two gunshots cracked through the air. Shouts. Screams. Two state policemen grabbed Jess and rushed her down the stairs.

Some in the crowd were frozen in place. Some gaped and moved around. Some sobbed and grabbed their loved ones. Some rushed to their cars.

They hadn't been gunshots, of course. They'd been the kind of firecrackers designed to scare folks into *believing* they were gunshots.

A state officer was now reassuring the crowd that the congresswoman was safe, number one, and, number two, that somebody who would soon be found had set off two firecrackers.

As a matter of fact, another state man dragging a skinny man in a dirty white shirt way too thin for the temperature appeared and basically flung the man into the arms of another state man. Out came the cuffs and a violent shove in the direction of the state police cars.

Now that I could see him in some detail he resembled a poster icon for meth addicts. Even from a distance I could see that the cheeks had caved in and that the eyes had the zombie look that could frighten even old pros. He was screaming: 'I was just foolin' around! I was just foolin' around!'

A half-ass DA could make the case that he had endangered lives in several ways, not least by risking the health of the elderly present tonight. People with heart problems could suffer an attack or even death.

But forget the half-ass mythical DA. I was worried as a campaign manager that this sad, crazed creature had stepped on our message tonight. Would the TV news spend more time on the screaming, terrified crowd than they would on the message we'd carefully crafted over the phone ninety minutes before Jess left the house to come here? We'd thrown out the speech we'd planned and decided that while it was all right to complain that we'd been set up, doing that risked turning Jess into a whiner. Invoking the Justice Department showed that we not only proclaimed innocence, we demanded that it be proven.

The hitch of course, which both Dorsey and the smarter reporters would point out, was that getting the Justice Department interested would likely take some time – if they ever got interested at all. But now we were on the offensive and making at least some average citizens wonder if Dorsey and his associates might not be behind this.

When Jess returned to the microphone it was easy to tell in her voice and posture that the firecrackers had shaken her.

'I remember when Bobby Kennedy said not long before his assassination that if they wanted to kill you, they would. I'm begin-ning to see what he meant.' She was recovering quickly. 'Now it's family time, everybody. Time to get home on a cold night like this one. And if you don't have a family, I hope you at least have a cat or a dog.' Laughter. 'Over the years my cats have given me a lot of comfort.' Then, in a gush, 'Thank you so much for coming here tonight. Even those of you in the back who don't like me – I thank you, too. Standing around in the cold listening to me – well, there are a lot better things to do than that.'

More affectionate laughter. No boos this time.

'Good night, everybody. Stay safe!'

She walked inside the bears again. The sharpshooter on the bandstand redoubled his stance and his scan of every inch of ground his eyes were capable of assessing.

Then Jess was in the police caravan and headed back to the family manse.

Abby was beside me now. 'I can't believe how well this went. Except for the firecrackers, I mean. I hope they put him in a cell with a homicidal maniac.'

'I'll bet you didn't learn that from the nuns.'

'You'd be surprised what I learned at Catholic school.'

'I probably would be.'

She laid her head against my arm. 'God, we've worked so hard on this one. And it all just came crashing down.'

'It's not over yet. And the press should be having sex, they're so happy with tonight.' I didn't mention the possibility that they'd let the firecrackers overwhelm the message. Then, 'Feel like getting a drink?'

'I wish I could.' Abby was sliding away from me now. 'But I have an actual date.'

'Well, it was bound to happen to one of us.' I leaned down and kissed her on the cheek. 'Good luck, Abby. It's your turn.'

Not too long after I was in my hotel room in my boxers and T-shirt, checking out my other campaigns. My phone rang just before eleven o'clock. Karen Foster.

'I hope I didn't wake you up.'

'I'm glad to hear your voice.'

'Well, I'm glad to hear *yours*. So there.'

'You home?'

'Yep, and in my jammies watching Jimmy Fallon.' Then, 'I wanted to invite you for dinner tomorrow.'

'Well, thank you. I look forward to it.'

'I have to tell you I've had a number of bad relationships in my life so I'm kind of nervous about putting myself out there again, but you seem like a very nice guy.'

'I don't know about that, but I like it when we're together. I'm not only attracted to you, I admire you. You're another very rare species of human being.'

'Yeah? What's that?'

'A tough cookie. You're going to get Showalter no matter what.'

'I didn't do a very good job when he murdered my stepbrother.'

'He's smart and he's ruthless and he protects himself with his badge. That makes him a difficult target.'

'Maybe with both of us working on it—' She yawned. And laughed. 'I've learned that to get a man in the proper mood for seduction, yawning really works.'

'No argument here. Just the one yawn and I started tearing my clothes off right away.'

'Well, I don't want to get you worked up any more than you already are, so I'll just say goodnight. Oh, let me give you my address and landline number. Let's say seven o'clock.'

She might not have wanted me to get worked up, but worked up I was. I had a very nice wild dream about her. About us.

THIRTY-TWO

There were two press conferences in the morning.

Mike Edelstein had invited a print reporter and two TV teams to our campaign office where he sat behind a long table with a slender, middle-aged bald man in a blue button-down shirt. This, Edelstein said, was Tim Rosencrantz from Chicago, who had testified in numerous trials as a lock-and-key forensics expert.

He'd told me yesterday about this presentation. I had to admit that I'd never heard of a lock-and-key forensics expert. Few in the home audience would have either, making Mr Rosencrantz all the more interesting.

That morning he briefly set the scene, recalling the night of the gunshots and the police discovery of the rifle in Cory Tucker's trunk.

Edelstein said, 'The police claim that Cory Tucker's trunk lock had not been tampered with. This was supposed to mean, I guess, that there was no chance that the rifle had been planted in his car trunk. I found this conclusion to be rash and reckless, so I consulted with Mr Rosencrantz here. I'll let him take it from here.'

Rosencrantz had duplicated the exact kind of lock Cory had on his trunk. He held it in his hand and turned it over and over slowly so the cameras could get good shots of it.

He then took out a presentation folder that had large drawings of the lock. He flipped through them as he spoke. 'If a person doesn't understand how to examine a lock in detail he can easily conclude that it hasn't been picked. Picking tools are usually made out of aluminum or iron or steel and are very thin. But thin as they are – and as competent as the lock pick may be – the pick and the tension of opening the lock leave marks such as gouges and scratches. You need somebody familiar with lock-and-key forensics to determine this.'

Rosencrantz had flipped through the drawings as he'd spoken. Damn, he was good. Edelstein was a believer in shorter-is-better. Rosencrantz spoke only one time and then it was back to Mike.

'Since Chief Showalter was so eager to claim that Cory Tucker's trunk lock had not been tampered with I ask him now – publicly – to let our expert examine the lock with the chief and a few of his officers in attendance. He can always say wait until the run-up to the trial when he has to turn all evidence over to us. But I say in the interest of fairness let us do it right now, and I believe this will make it clear that there will be no need for a trial. That Cory Tucker was set up. That somebody from the opposing side of this election planted that rifle in his trunk.'

Edelstein had laughed about this being a 'suicide run.' Jess had all but accused Dorsey of setting up the entire staged shooting, and now Mike had just directly alluded to the 'opposing side.' The public was either going to buy our act or not. All we needed was half of them.

The war was on and I was enjoying the hell out of it once again.

Jess's press conference was longer.

She was in the public room of a Methodist church where a group of Iraq and Afghanistan vets met every Monday and Friday. By now Americans have seen so many injured vets that for the most part the shock of seeing a man or woman without legs or arms has lessened somewhat. Somewhat. But then there is the man whose face has been burned into a horrific mask. Or the woman whose lips are little more than slits. Or the man who shakes every five minutes or so as if he's having a seizure. The shock of seeing these people has not lessened at all.

We'd fashioned a good standard speech for Jess about the plight of our vets. You can get too angry or sentimental and dull the impact of the issue. After allowing for outrage, we went to statistics and biography. We told the stories of two typical National Guard soldiers who had been drafted into war for three tours. One man, one woman. From right here in Illinois. Both of them wounded on their final tour.

Jason Lindberg lost both of his legs in Afghanistan. The Veterans Administration did well by him at first. The surgery had gone as well as could be expected. The rehab program had also been helpful. What lagged was treatment for his mental issues. Both he and his wife pleaded for help but the only psychologists available were scheduled months out. Eighteen months after his return home Jason swallowed half a bottle of prescription antidepressants and died. His wife Jan was at work and returned to find him dead in his wheelchair.

Caitlin Scalise was a divorced woman who had been in the guard since college. After being shot in the chest three times she learned through surgery that her heart was not functioning properly. The paperwork delays were so extreme she died of a heart attack before the VA scheduled her for an appointment.

'I don't want to belong to a party that votes against increasing financial help for our veterans. And I'm sure none of my friends here do either.'

You can't miss with cops, soldiers or nuns standing behind you when you're speaking. I once suggested to an especially randy client of mine that he should have all the hookers he'd paid for over the years behind him. He was not greatly amused but then neither was I. In the middle of a close campaign (his aide had told me this) he'd spent two hours in a massage parlor that all but promised 'happy endings' right on the front window. A wise, wise man.

The four reporters present were nice enough to ask Jess how she would remedy this terrible situation. Oddly enough, she had a few points prepared. All it lacked was some patriotic music and a couple hundred people saluting the flag.

Two very nice scores for us.

Cindy Fletcher called just as I was leaving for lunch.

'When Marie got home this morning she said she was sure somebody had gotten in here between the time I left for work and she got home. I left work so I could look things over.'

Marie worked the night shift at the hospital where Cindy worked the day shift. Marie's was now her hiding place.

'What makes her think so?'

'Well, for one thing it rained last night and the ground around the stairs – she lives in the upper apartment – was real muddy. There's a muddy footprint just outside her door. And the rubber mat she has outside the door shows where mud was wiped off. There's a – what's the word? – imprint of a man's shoe on the mat. A very large imprint. Inside on the living-room rug there's a little piece of mud, and there's one in the little room where I'm staying too. Like he didn't get all the mud off but didn't realize it.

'My room's tiny. It's only got a small closet and a single bed and a window. I keep my suitcase in the closet but when she got home it was on my bed and open. And like I said – a small piece of mud on the floor there, too.'

'They think you have the recorder.'

'I wish I did. I'd give it to them and get this over with. I just want Granddad to be safe.'

'They've focused on Grimes and you.'

'Like I said, I just want it over with. I don't even care about it anymore. I wish Dave hadn't recorded anything.'

I thought of Karen Foster. Only with the recorder could she bring down Showalter. The recorder would give her justice and the recorder would tell me who had ordered the staged assassination attempt. We both had urgent reasons to find it.

'It really scares me – somebody coming in here like that. Like they could do it any time they want to. Marie's probably thinking twice now about having me stay here. I'll probably have to start looking for someplace else to stay now.'

'I'll handle that.'

'Marie's over at her cousin's. She just wanted to get out of here. And I can't say I blame her.'

She was upset enough that my words hadn't seemed to register.

'I'll find a place for you, Cindy. It's probably a good idea for you to get out of there, too.'

'I need to get back to work, anyway.'

'Good. By mid-afternoon I'll have a place for you to stay.'

'I appreciate all your help, Dev.'

'I'm being selfish, Cindy. If the recorder proves that Dorsey was involved in the staged shooting, we've cleared Jess's name and won the campaign.'

'Be selfish all you want. Just keep me safe.'

'I'll do my best.' But even as I spoke the words I knew I should have played Papa Bear. Sounded confident, even certain. 'You're going to be fine. And we're going to get that recorder.'

'God, I'm so glad you said that, Dev. Thank you so much.'

The rain started around three that afternoon – one of those blinding downpours that diminished spirits and grayed out a face even as vivid as Abby's.

Jean Fellows had arranged to house Cindy for a few days with the proviso that she had an entire season of *Downton Abbey* and would permit only that to decorate her screen when she got home after work. If Cindy didn't like that, 'She can read the *National Enquirer* or something.' The slashing rain hadn't done much for Jean's mood, either. She'd intended her remark as a joke, but there had been an edge to it.

The Dorsey campaign had fielded a new theme: 'Trust is all that matters.' I had the radio on so I could hear the first two spots they were running. Nothing surprising and the same kind of thing we'd have done in Dorsey's position.

I had the teenage notion that Karen Foster would surprise me with a phone call. A little reminder of what was on the menu tonight and how she hoped I was as happy in my anticipation as she was. I kept glancing at the clock on my desk. I even called it a dirty name once. I was far too mature to give it the finger.

The day ended with some new internal numbers that were not quite as bad as I'd feared they'd be. According to our own people we were now four points behind. We had another debate to go and

Dorsey's campaign always had to fear that he would say something intemperate, such as (this was one of his best) unwed teenage mothers should have to register in order to bring back 'shame' into our society. 'Shame' would make our culture what it used to be, he said. He was probably right. The Salem Witch Trials certainly worked pretty well with shame propelling them.

By the time I drove back to my hotel the rain was little more than a drizzle but the sky was a roiling blackish-gray and the sound of thunder was steady and ominous.

I did fifty pushups, shaved again, showered and put on a fresh white T-shirt, a tan V-neck sweater and a pair of brown trousers. An actual date and I was excited about it. My daughter Sarah would be, too, when I emailed her the results. She wanted me to be married again. She was convinced that in wedded bliss I would be able to answer all the cosmic questions and riddles that had beleaguered mankind for millions of years. But with a fifty-percent divorce rate in this country, wedded bliss sure eluded a lot of couples.

THIRTY-THREE

Karen lived in a small New England-style cottage hidden behind a long hedge and surrounded by enormous oak trees. The address was clearly marked on a country-style mailbox out front, or I might not have been able to find it.

By now the downpour had returned. My wipers sliced back and forth as I followed the narrow concrete drive that ended adjacent to the house.

Light poured from the front window, welcoming given the rain pounding on my rental and the spider-legged lightning I saw in the distance.

As I passed the lone front window I glanced inside. Cozy. Tan carpeting, earth-toned walls and furnishings. A very small fireplace glowed as flame engulfed timber.

No sign of Karen.

I probably knocked harder than I needed to but when there was no response I assumed that she still hadn't heard me. Then I saw a tiny button of a doorbell and pushed it. I heard the sound peal inside. For no particular reason I stepped back over to the front window and looked in again. I really wanted to see her. But I didn't. I tried the bell again and again but got no response. I opened the exterior glass door and knocked hard on the wooden interior one. And the force of my knock pushed it back so that all I had to do was step inside.

'Karen! It's me, Dev!'

I stepped up over the threshold and called out again.

A certain kind of emptiness has a feel, a wrong feel. The lights, the fire, the unlocked door. She should have been in front of me by now. Maybe we should have even been making out a little, striking the start of our own kind of fire to get us through this drenched night that would be clogging up sewers and flooding the streets all too soon.

The wrong kind of emptiness. I started moving through the house.

As adult and occasionally fierce as she was, there was a gentleness to the decor that touched me. The large bedroom sheltered fanciful stuffed creatures of many kinds; the kitchen was bright and happy with framed drawings from Victorian-era children's books. I recognized them because my wife and daughter had loved them, too. No signs of a dinner being prepared.

She'd fashioned herself an office in the smallest room. Desk, computer and bookshelves filled with mysteries and a few romance novels. The desk lamp still shone, lending a noirish shadow to everything else.

There was a back porch. In the shadows I could see return cartons of Diet Pepsi cans. A pair of skis. I flipped on the light and checked for any traces of struggle. None. There was no garage. There was also no car. Lights on, fire going, desk lamp burning and car gone.

The wrong kind of emptiness.

I reversed my course and went back through the house room by room in case I'd missed some explanation of what may have happened to her.

But nothing.

I closed and locked the front door and walked out to my car to retrieve the flashlight. I spent the next ten minutes searching the grounds. The onslaught of rain didn't bother me much. She took precedence over the weather.

I wanted this to be a TV episode of a crime show. Man searching in the downpour for at least one clue to the disappearance of a missing woman. In my investigator days I was usually able to formulate an alternate plan when I ran out of ideas. The problem was that I didn't know anybody who knew her. Showalter would never tell me about her day, where she'd gone, what she'd done. As much as she wanted to put Showalter in prison – or on death row – she still had to report to him. So he wouldn't have any trouble finding her if he'd decided to end their professional relationship violently.

Then I remembered Bromfield and the cop bar.

They didn't look any happier to see me than they had the other night.

In fact, when Henry saw me he reached down, grabbed his ball bat and set it right on the bar so I'd be sure to see it. He made sure to pop his biceps.

The scene was the same, too. Girlfriends and groupies and the younger cops; the more sedate married pairs. The ones who stared at me the longest were the loners. I didn't see Bromfield.

'Get out,' Henry said as I approached the bar.

'I was wondering if I'd find Showalter in here.'

'You got big hairy ones, I've got to give you that. 'Course, they may not be attached to your body much longer once I get through with this bat.'

I tried to make my scan of the place casual. I didn't see Bromfield anywhere. Then he pulled a Clint Eastwood. He shoved the bat across the bar and into my chest. 'Now get the hell out of here.'

He had now gotten the attention he wanted. We were in another D-minus Western movie written and directed by Henry. And starring Henry as well.

A semicircle of aftershave- and cologne-wearing off-duty cops and a bully boy with a bat glaring at me.

To my right, I saw the door of the office in back open up. I heard 'Your turn to deal, Stan.' And then I saw Bromfield leaving the office, laughing and saying over his shoulder, 'Now I don't even have enough money for any meth. I'm going home.'

He had a surprised expression when he saw me. Probably wondered why I'd been crazed enough to come back here. But he picked up his cue immediately.

'What's this asshole doin' here, Henry?'

'Ask him.'

'I'm looking for Chief Showalter.'

Bromfield played it out. 'Showalter?' His eyes scanned his fellow officers. 'When he's pissed he's one of the scariest guys I've ever seen. Even Henry here's afraid of Showalter – even when Henry's got his ball bat. Just be glad he *isn't* here, jerk-off. Otherwise you'd be on the floor. In pieces.'

Now it was my turn to look at them. There was no way to tell if any of them belonged to Showalter's group. But this was *their* place, invitation only. And I definitely wasn't the type who'd get himself invited.

I shrugged. 'Guess I'll be leaving now.'

'Wise decision,' Bromfield said.

Henry slapped bat against palm again. He needed a new writer. Bad.

I was plum out of smart lines to accompany my retreat. All I did was shrug, turn around and head for the front door.

And hope that Bromfield – who'd been damned convincing, come to think of it – would join me down the block where I'd parked.

The chill rain was little more than a drizzle now.

The ancient ruins of the deserted buildings on both sides of the street lent the night a feeling of despair. Their lives were over and soon enough they would be utterly gone, like the people who had filled them with the day-to-day joys and sorrows of life.

I leaned against my car waiting for Bromfield to show up. I might be waiting forever if he'd decided helping me out would lead to trouble for him. Maybe serious trouble.

I watched the way the raindrops sparkled off the metal hoods of the old streetlamps. They were having a much better time than I was.

He pulled up behind me with his headlights off. Now he wore a black-hooded rain jacket. The hood was pulled so far up I couldn't see much of his face.

'Henry's going to use that ball bat on you next time you go in there.'

'No "next time" for me. I know when my luck's tapped out.'

'This could be real deep shit for me, Conrad. You got a question, you better ask it, and fast.'

'You notice anything different about Showalter's behavior the last day or so?'

He'd managed to cup his hand around a cigarette and light it. Two cars splashed by but the puddles were thin and they weren't going fast.

'How'd you know about that?'

'I may be onto something. My guess is he's acting pretty strange. Preoccupied.'

'He's yelling at us a lot, something he doesn't do very often. Oh, and this afternoon I guess he caught Karen Foster in his office. He was supposed to be testifying in court most of the afternoon and came back early. I hear you know Karen.'

Heartburn and a queasy feeling in my lower stomach. 'Yeah. I know Karen.'

'Showalter sure didn't like that. You and her, I mean.'

She had pushed it too far. It hadn't been bright, sneaking into his office that way.

'The secretary had this dental appointment. I guess she must have thought it was safe.'

'How did it end up?'

'The secretary got back just in time to hear her scream at him that she was resigning. Then she walked straight out of the station.'

'You happen to see or hear from her?'

'Nah. We're not big buds or anything. But I'll tell you one thing. She's the smartest person in the whole place.'

We both heard it down the block. The front door of Batter Up opening and a small flood of people laughing boozily, coming out into the night.

'I gotta get out of here.'

'You got a cell phone I could call you on if I needed to?'

'For what?'

'Could you use two hundred dollars?'

'Are you kidding? You know the kind of shit salary a cop in this town makes?'

He got two crisp one-hundred-dollar bills and I got a cell number.

PART FOUR

THIRTY-FOUR

Except for when my father died, I'd never been in a hospital this late at night. The front part, not the ER.

So quiet. And no medicinal smells whatsoever. Enormous photographs of medical giants down the centuries hung from the lobby walls, which had been refurbished. The expensive, comfortable furnishings were new, as was the large glassed-in office with ADMISSIONS on the door where a lone woman was busy working on her computer. She heard me approach and looked up with a smile. 'Good evening.'

'Hi. I'm just here checking up on a friend of mine.'

'Oh?'

'Karen Foster.'

'Oh. Miss Foster.' The smile remained but the voice bore a hint of concern. 'She's been in surgery for the past three hours. I'm afraid she still is.'

'The radio said she was in critical condition.'

'I'm afraid she is.' She was an attractive woman, probably in her early fifties. The gray-streaked hair in a tight bun, the inexpensive gray suit still well chosen and well suited to her upper body.

'I know she doesn't have any relatives in town. Has anybody asked about her?'

'Well, there's an annoying reporter who calls every twenty minutes.'

'Anybody else?'

'Not "inquiring" about her as such. But the night supervisor told me that two police officers are standing outside the surgery room and were outside her room on the fourth floor.'

With absolutely no proof but well-grounded suspicion, I played out a quick scenario. A Showalter cop follows her up into the hills after she leaves the office. The dark. The rain. Slams into her hard enough to push her off the road. The descent was supposed to be violent enough to kill her. But she didn't have the decency to die. Showalter had to be afraid now. If she could survive she could talk.

And even if nobody believed her, she would be able – and willing now – to tell the story about Showalter and his bank-robbing patriotic cops.

Showalter was not going to let that happen.

'Do you mind if I ask you a question, sir?'

'No. Of course not.'

'Did I see you on TV the other night talking about Congresswoman Bradshaw?'

'Yes, you did. My name's Dev Conrad. I'm her campaign manager.'

'Both my daughter and I are volunteers. I do what I can with the hours I have but my daughter goes to her campaign headquarters right after school three or four days a week.' Then, 'I think she's still going to win. My husband worked at a place that Dorsey owned. Terrible place. They held out for better wages and better working conditions and he pulled a lockout. Fired them all, across the board, even some of them who'd been there thirty years, long before he'd bought it.'

'He's a piece of work.'

'He was behind that fake shooting attempt, wasn't he?'

She answered my smile with her own.

'You're not going to say it out loud but I know you believe it, too.'

I was thinking about Karen's car. Specifically the rear bumper. 'Do you know where they take cars that have been pretty badly damaged after an accident like Karen's?'

'Well, the towing company's name is Watson's Garage. He gets all the police business because his uncle is a friend of Chief Showalter's. I suppose that's where it is. That's three blocks east of the station.'

'You've been very helpful, thanks.'

'My pleasure.'

'Would you mind if I called in a little while to check on Karen's condition?'

'I'll be happy to help you but I'd give it another hour at least.'

'Thanks again.'

I walked back out into the rain. I started my car but didn't put it in gear. I just sat there continuing to go over the little information the radio story had divulged at some length.

Sometime just after dusk, Karen's car had skidded off a narrow road up on top of one of those steep limestone cliffs in the eastern rural part of the town. A passerby had noticed a stray beam of light angling up from the creek far below the cliff. He'd gotten out of the car to see what had happened and inched his way down in the stinging downpour. He'd related all this to the reporter in excited tones. The car had been crushed in on itself from rolling over two or three times. He said he'd seen a woman trapped inside. There was no way he could extract her. He'd brought a flashlight with him. From what he could see of her bloody face, he'd assumed she was dead. He'd called 911. They'd needed the jaws of life to extract her. He'd been surprised to hear the ambulance tech say she was still alive.

I spent five minutes more thinking about my scenario. Unless it really had been an accident there weren't many alternate ways Karen's car could have been sent down the side of a steep cliff.

The tone of my cell phone brought me out of my speculating.

'It's Bromfield.'

'You going to earn your two hundred?'

'I just wanted to make sure you'd heard about Karen Foster.'

'Yeah, I have. In fact, I'm in the hospital parking lot. She's been in surgery for three hours.'

'I'm doubting you think this was an accident.'

'Do you?'

'Hell, no, I don't. And neither do a couple of the other officers I talked to tonight. One of them said that Showalter's out at the casino pouring them down.'

'What kind of car does Karen drive?'

'Silver Camry, a couple years old.'

'Is it hard to get into Watson's?'

'Not if you're a cop.'

'Think I could get sworn in right away?'

'No, but I can meet you there in about twenty minutes. You know how to get there?'

'Three blocks east of the station?'

'Right. See you there.'

I'd paid him way too little. If Showalter ever found out he'd helped me to this extent, Bromfield would be out of a job. Or given what Showalter had probably done to Karen tonight, he could lose a lot more.

THIRTY-FIVE

Watson's Garage turned out to be part salvage yard, part repair shop, part gas station. Even this late at night mechanics were working in the bays and the open office door was noisy with rap music and yellow light.

I waited in my car just inside the drive. I assumed that before they let me examine the car Bromfield would have to introduce me.

Bromfield showed up about ten minutes after I arrived. He beeped and waved me on to follow him. We ended up parking directly across from the office.

As I got out of my car, the air was rich with the scents of gasoline, motor oil, welding and that accrued mixed aroma of dying and death peculiar to metal beings consigned to salvage yards.

Watson's was prosperous enough to have two large, long trucks of the flatbed variety sitting side by side near the wall of cyclone fencing.

'This is a big operation,' I said.

'You can grow fast when the city council gives you all its business.'

'That's what the woman at the hospital told me.'

'If the state boys ever spent any time here seeing how this place is really run there'd be a whole lot of people doing a perp walk, believe me.' Then, 'This shouldn't be any problem. Bobby Marie works the night shift. She's the female equivalent of the good ol' boy, right down to the chewing tobacco.'

'Wow.'

He laughed. 'Yeah. Wow. And she likes rap music.'

I was still trying to process all these warring personality elements when we stepped inside and I saw a peroxided thirty-something woman with an enormous bosom packed into a pink T-shirt with the photograph of a rapper on it. She was actually pretty, in a kind of fierce way. The makeup had been put on with a paint roller and the T-shirt was ready to burst, but if you just focused on the large blue eyes you saw intelligence and kindness, even if the cobra tat on her left arm said otherwise.

The rap music was deafening.

Bromfield had to half shout. 'How's your little girl, Bobby Marie?'

'I'm thinkin' of putting her in another one of those tiny tot beauty pageants.'

I'd once seen a documentary on those things. How the producers of the shows ripped off the parents and how the parents – especially the mothers – turned their innocent little daughters into frightened participants in a nightmare of exploitation. Mothers screaming at their daughters when they didn't perform well; mothers even *slapping* already neurotic and scared little daughters.

I had my nice liberal speech all ready to go, but I decided that this probably wasn't the best time to give it.

Then, 'Just a sec.' She turned the music way down. 'Who's he?'

'A friend of mine.'

'He got a name?'

'Dev Conrad,' I said.

'You a cop, too?'

'Afraid not.'

A true cackle. 'Good, 'cause I can't stand cops.' To Bromfield, 'So what can I do you for, Officer?'

'Just wanted to check out a car that was brought here earlier tonight.'

'That'd have to be that Foster gal's. Only one we've had all day we had to tow.'

'So I'd just like to look it over.'

'Why?'

'Why? You trying to bust my chops, Bobby Marie?'

'No can do. Got orders that nobody sees it.'

'Orders? From who?'

'The boss. Gil called me even before they brought it in. Said Showalter called and said nobody was allowed to inspect it. And he meant nobody. Little Bobby Marie's smart enough to know when the man who owns the place tells you nobody inspects it, I need to make sure that nobody inspects it.'

'I've never heard of this before.'

'Tell you the truth, neither have I. And I admit it's kind of weird, but right now there isn't a damned thing I can do about it.'

Bromfield shrugged and looked at me.

I shrugged right back.

Bromfield said, 'Bobby Marie, you sure you couldn't just give us a couple of minutes to look it over?'

'Oh, I could. But the old man's scared he's gonna get laid off and my little daughter's next pageant dress is gonna cost me a lot more than the last one, so I just can't take a chance. If my old man gets laid off and Gil decides to fire my ass, my whole family's in a world of hurt.'

I said, 'Well, we appreciate your time. Sorry you can't help us.'

Suspicion colored her voice for the first time. 'Gil said somebody from Congresswoman Bradshaw's campaign might stop by and try to see it. And right now I'm betting you're that man.'

'Yeah, I am.'

'Well, mister, it's nothing personal but you best scat out of here. Soon as you're gone I have to call Gil and tell him you were here.'

We ended on that cackle of hers. 'I'd say Showalter don't like you too much, you know what I'm sayin'?'

When we were walking to our cars, Bromfield said, 'Man, Showalter's got this town sewed up tight. Bobby Marie isn't usually scared of anybody.'

'It's time I talk with Showalter.'

'What do you mean?'

'I mean I'm going out to the casino and calling him out on it. It's way past time.'

He caught my elbow. 'That's a trip I can't afford to take.'

'I know.' My smile was intended to make us both feel better. 'But I'm sure you'll hear all about it.'

THIRTY-SIX

C asinos always remind me of being on cruise ships. They are self-contained and claustrophobic, filled with amusements that almost always disappoint. And if you're not careful they can be dangerous.

Another point: they take as their icon Las Vegas, Nevada.

I'm occasionally dragged out there for a convention. There was even one would-be client who wanted to meet in Vegas. I backed out two days before the meeting. Vegas was bad vibes.

The Empire Casino was standard stuff. Just inside the four glass doors there was a long list of all the gaming machines (twelve hundred in total) and table and poker games (thirty total). There were, in addition, five hundred seats for bingo.

There was an area for eating, a food court, a café, a buffet and a steak and seafood joint.

The hotel boasted three hundred and seventy-four rooms and fifteen suites.

I followed a theater-like lobby into rows of slots clamorous with the various sounds of humans dealing with machines that wouldn't obey.

The female employees, if not quite as leggy or pretty or poised as their Las Vegas sisters, were nonetheless attractive and appealing and, as always, I wondered how the hell they could keep smiling as long as they did and put up with all the inevitable drunken male bullshit that went with any gig like this. My daughter had been a waitress between her sophomore and junior years in college. A decent place. But man, the tales she told. I wanted to go down there with a bullwhip.

I wound my way along the blackjack tables, the roulette tables and the mini-baccarat setup, which was surprisingly busy.

If nothing else, casinos are democratic. Every race, creed and sex demonstrate their eagerness to lose their asses to the house.

There were four poker tables set in a small wing of the place. Five players at each. Showalter was at the nearest table. He could easily have seen me if he'd looked up from the card the dealer had just dealt. But he was too busy scowling. Apparently he was not having a good time.

He threw his cards down on the table and shook his head with real disgust. And then, as if we'd connected telepathically, his eyes raised and met mine.

He was a champion scowler, our police chief was; this one was his deepest yet.

He wasted no time. He shoved his chair back and stood up. I couldn't hear what he said but obviously the other players didn't want to see him go. Maybe because he was the chief and it was sort of cool playing with him, or maybe because he was such a shitty player he was giving them part of his kids' college fund.

He came straight at me. He wore a tweed sport jacket, white shirt, no tie and gray trousers. He also wore a look of real menace, enough to make me wonder if coming here had been such a good idea. Mike Edelstein could bail me out in a few hours if Showalter decided to arrest me. But he couldn't do much until it was too late to help me if Showalter decided to take me down to the station and see that I was beaten.

'I don't want you here, Conrad.'

'You own the place?'

'No. But I know the manager here and he doesn't want any undesirables.'

'Yeah, undesirables in a casino would really be a bad thing.'

The grip on my elbow made me grit my teeth. I didn't want to show pain.

'Now's the time to leave, Conrad.'

'I want to get a look at Karen Foster's car. The one you ran off the road tonight.'

His hand fell away from my elbow and the scowl became one of his sneering smiles.

'That's what you came out here for?'

'That and wanting to know what you did with Grimes.'

'You know if I was a private citizen I'd be filing lawsuits against you every day of the week. Libel and slander.'

'And for setting up that fake shooting with Congresswoman Bradshaw.'

He leaned back. I had the feeling that he'd never really assessed me before. The way a cop does, I mean. He was doing it now.

Sounds of the casino crowded in as he stood there in silence examining me.

'You're really trying to nail my ass, aren't you?'

'Karen Foster may not make it.'

'You want me to act all worried and sad? She got the job under false pretenses. I started getting suspicious when a couple of my men saw her with you.' So he had discovered her real identity and purpose in coming to Danton.

'She's been trying to nail my ass, too. Just like you. I'm not surprised you two got together. Hell, she may have brought you here, for all I know.'

He was coming undone. I hadn't heard that in him until just

now. Big bad Showalter was starting to feel the pressure. He was beginning to realize that badge and gun could protect you only so far.

'She didn't bring me here. She brought herself here. Because she knows who you really are and what you've done.'

A security guard strode into sight with the aplomb of a big, battered man who learned long ago that sight of him would put most men and women on alert. But then there was, as now, that almost demented smile. Maybe he was comic relief on this ship to nowhere.

Every casino has got at least three of them. Somebody gets unruly, somebody tries to cheat the house, somebody just really pisses off the managers . . . and out comes one of these guys. Showalter was royalty here.

Maybe somebody watching on the cameras on the second floor saw how upset I made Showalter and he contacts King Kong and tells him to run this guy's ass out of here.

He stood next to Showalter and said, 'I was watching you from across the way there. And if I didn't know better, I'd say that you're giving one of our preferred customers here a whole raft of shit.'

He jabbed a finger half the size of Henry's ball bat into my chest.

'In which case, I have to say that you don't belong here. If you had any idea of how much this man has done for this town and for me personally, you'd be shaking his hand right now just because he's—'

'That's enough, Billy. But thank you. Conrad here was not only accusing me of various things I had nothing to do with, he was also refusing to leave, even though I had told him politely that I'd appreciate it if he did.'

Quite an act they had here. Showalter had his old self-confidence back. He was the cool guy once again.

'Is that true? The chief here asked you to leave and you wouldn't?'

'I want to see Karen Foster's car, Showalter. Have a claims adjuster look it over.' But I knew that was it.

Billy started moving in on me. 'Oh, he'll leave, all right. Or he'll be sorry.'

This time when Billy jabbed me, he did so with enough power to push me back a couple of inches.

'I'm givin' you one more chance,' Billy said. 'You understand?' And understand I did.

THIRTY-SEVEN

At this time of night, the parking lot of the Skylight tavern had only three cars gracing its busted asphalt surface. I swung the rental into a slot and went inside.

There were three men along the bar, two at one of the wobbly tables. The bartender recognized me with no particular expression. He wore a blue short-sleeved shirt and a white smeared apron.

The Eugene O'Neill ambience was there even without a full contingent of lost souls. Generations of loss and failure and fear soaked the place physically and spiritually.

The men at the bar weren't even talking. Just sitting there drinking and staring. The bartender continued watching me silently as I walked over to him.

'Grimes been around?'

'Haven't seen him.'

He didn't react but a pair of the older men sitting at the bar did. They seemed to be surprised that he'd said what he had.

'Hell, tell him what happened,' a hawk-faced, gray-haired man said. The hawk visage was enhanced by the eyes. In the worn, elderly face they shone with intelligence and cunning. He laughed through a spell of cigarette hacking. 'Haven't seen Grimes move that fast in a long time.'

'Shut the hell up, Patton,' the man next to him said. 'There's nothin' wrong with Grimes. He's in some kind of trouble and we shouldn't be laughin' about it.'

'He say what kind of trouble he was in?' I asked the small man with the charitable, sad eyes of a man who drank to buffer himself against the worst of the world.

Now the bartender spoke up. 'He was looking for a gun. Said he needed one for protection.'

The man called Patton said, 'I saw you walk back to the office with him. You were in there long enough to give him one.'

'Shut the hell up,' the bartender said.

'Grimes was half nuts. I sure wouldn't have given him a gun.'

'That's my business, not yours, Patton.'

To the bartender I said, 'Grimes's granddaughter is terrified because we can't find him. Think we could step back in that office and talk a little?'

'Cindy's a sweetheart, Hal. You should talk to this guy.'

Patton started to say something but I clamped my hand on the back of his neck and squeezed hard. 'Shut the fuck up. You understand?'

One of the men at the table said, 'Kick his ass, man. He's had it comin' a long time.'

'C'mon,' Hal said.

The office was a collection of ancient girly calendars, two wooden filing cabinets, a desk with one leg propped up by a phone book and an adding machine you probably hadn't been able to buy parts for in several decades. There were two chairs. Neither of us sat.

'He was in Nam. With me.'

'Grimes?'

'Yeah. We were good buddies and still are. You go through a war with somebody, you don't forget about them.'

'So you gave Grimes a gun?'

'Old Colt I got from my old man.'

'Loaded?'

'Yeah. He was so scared I figure he needed it.'

'What did Patton mean about Grimes moving so fast?'

'He was so scared he jumped at everything. He heard a siren and he just ran out of here. Knocked over his glass on the bar and broke it while he was at it. I felt sorry for him. A lot of people don't like him. But like I say, we went through Nam together.'

'Any idea where he went?'

'No.' He nodded to the door. 'I don't trust Patton. I better get out there.'

'I appreciate the information.'

'I just hope he's all right.'

'Yeah,' I said. 'Me, too.'

THIRTY-EIGHT

The hotel bar stayed open until midnight.

Tonight I didn't find any middle-aged female counterpart to comfort my roiled state of mind. The first thing I did was call the hospital to get an update on Karen. She was in a stable condition.

There were two calls on my cell pertaining to two other races.

One was good news, one bad.

The other man at the bar wanted to talk politics with the bartender, but she laughed and said that from what he'd been telling her last night he'd better be careful because sitting two stools away was none other than the dreaded congresswoman's campaign manager.

The guy was two drinks shy of belligerence, so I shoved off and went up to my room, where I fell asleep much faster than I would have thought possible.

I dreamed about the shooting again, except this time it was for real. This time Jess's head wrenched around and gaped at me. Then the bullets struck the back of her skull. But as blood and pieces of her brain bloomed in the air above her head, she started laughing. The laugh, unlike a sound I'd ever heard before, was more disturbing than the violence had been.

Why was she laughing? I was never to find out.

The call was from a man whose voice was the human equivalent of a dangerous bridge. Very old. Unsteady. 'Is this Mr Conrad?'

The nightstand digital clock read six minutes after one a.m.

'Yes.'

'My name's Skully. I run River Cabins.'

'River Cabins?'

'Yeah. Along the river out to the west side.'

'I see.'

The nightmare had made more sense than this call. Skully? River Cabins? One in the morning? What the hell was this about?

'I've got an envelope for you.'

'What kind of envelope?'

'Just a plain white business one with your name on it.'

'Why do you have an envelope with my name on it?'

'Because he gave it to me.'

The 'he' gave me focus. I knew not to lose patience now. I swung around in bed and put my feet on the floor. The old habit of fumbling around for my pack of cigarettes came back to me. All these years and I still wanted one.

'You know a man named Grimes?'

'Yes, I do.'

'Well, that's why I'm calling.'

I cleared my throat. This was now an official call. This was a man who could lead me to Grimes. At least, that was the feeling I had.

'Is he with you right now?'

He might not have heard me. He didn't answer my question. 'Well, I don't want to get mixed up in nothin' so I thought I'd call you.'

'Mixed up in what? Mr Skully, I really need you to be more specific about things.'

'He left me this envelope with your name on it and the address of the hotel there. He said that if anything happened to him I was to get this to you.'

Whatever was going on, Cindy sure wasn't going to be happy about it.

'Is he there now in one of your cabins?'

'I think so.'

'You're not sure?'

'He was so jittery he might've taken off. He had a handgun. Soon as I seen it I knew I didn't want no part of it. But I took the envelope 'cause I was scared not to.'

The bartender's gun.

Worse and worse and worse. I'd been thinking that Grimes had just gotten scared and was hiding out. But the envelope made me wonder if he was up to something else only he could concoct.

'Where exactly are you located, Mr Skully?'

He told me. I'd need to program the GPS. 'Do you have phones in the cabins?'

'No.'

'I appreciate the call, Mr Skully.'

'I don't want any trouble. You have trouble and your name gets on TV and people don't want to come out here no more.'

'I understand. I'll be there as soon as I can.'

'You don't bring any guns, either, you hear me?'

'I hear you, Mr Skully. I hear you.'

I realized that I'd be waking Cindy up, but she needed to be told. She was more asleep than awake when she answered. ''Lo.'

'It's Dev. I may have located your grandfather.'

'Oh, God. Is he all right?'

I explained to her about the bartender giving him the gun and the old man calling me about her grandfather renting a cabin.

'Oh, God. They're pits. They've been closed down several times over the years. They're not even cabins. More like little garages. They were built during the Depression. Probably all he could afford.' Then, 'But why would he do this?'

'My guess is he didn't think it through. He got so excited about naming his price to Showalter that he didn't realize that there was no way Showalter could leave him alive. Now he's hiding from him.'

'Oh, God, poor Granddad. I know he sounds terrible doing this, but I love him so much and I'm so afraid for him. I can't help it, Dev.'

'I know that. I'm going to do my best to find him and protect him.'

'Just please call me and let me know what's going on.'

'I will, Cindy. As soon as I've got some news.'

I stuffed the Glock and the flashlight into the large interior pockets of my rain jacket. I also grabbed my thermos.

On my way out to Skully's I stopped long enough at a Hardee's to get my thermos filled.

Whatever the hell Grimes was up to, I was pretty sure he was going to make this a long and terrible night.

THIRTY-NINE

A wooden sign standing next to the narrow two-lane highway announced River Cabins, and in the heavy growth of pines far down the slope to the river you could see the outlines of cabins no bigger than a small garage.

Depression times came to mind. Poor people dragging themselves across the land in search of work probably stayed in places like these. And back then they would probably have been glad to have gotten them. They were preferable to sleeping outside in the rain and snow. And if you did it right you could probably pack a family of five or six inside them. There were migrant workers today in this home of the free and the brave who still lived this way.

Grimes's car was parked near the entrance behind a rusted dumpster.

A faded clapboard house sat just to the right of the sign. A lone light burned behind the dirty front window.

When I pulled in, a man in a red-and-white hunting jacket and a Cubs cap stepped out onto the porch. He had a handgun pointed straight at me. The welcoming committee.

'No need for that,' I said as I got out of my car.

'I'll be the judge of that.'

'I'm Conrad.'

'Makes no difference to me. I want you up here on the porch where I can see you. Grimes is so scared he's got me scared.'

'You hear from him?'

'Nope. Figured I'd wait for you to check his cabin. I don't like him havin' a gun.'

'Well, I'm not crazy about you having a gun, either.'

'Well, tough shit. I'm old and you're young. Figure the gun gives us some equality.'

When I walked up onto the porch the entire house shook. The recent rain had left the wood smelling of rot.

Skully's face in the window light was as weathered and woebegone as his home. He had a pair of quarter-sized growths on his left cheek that were light-colored and hairy. I wondered if he'd had a doctor look at them.

'You got some ID?'

'Sure.'

I dug in my back pocket for my wallet. The handgun – which turned out to be an old-fashioned .38 snubby – was still unerringly pointed at my chest. I handed it over and he managed to snatch it without losing his grip on the pistol.

He leaned back in the light to get a better look at my driver's license and that was when I saw that he had a third growth, just like the other two, on the right side of his neck. 'Yeah, I guess it's you all right.'

Who the hell else would it be?

'You have the envelope he left for me?'

He tapped the front of his hunting jacket. 'Right inside here.'

'You mind handing it over? And while you're at it, putting your gun away?'

A sigh. 'I should be inside in my bed right now 'stead of up all night with this kinda bullshit. If I don't get a good night's sleep I catch a cold. Soon as he showed me the envelope I shoulda kicked his ass out.'

But he slipped the gun into the wide pocket of his jacket and then reached inside and pulled out a white number-ten business envelope.

'It's all yours.'

It was so light there couldn't have been anything else besides a letter inside.

Then I felt the slight bump. Something maybe two inches long and a quarter inch thick, if that.

'Mind if I step over to the window there to read it?'

He didn't say anything, but he did step aside so I could move closer to the grimy light.

A single wooden stick match. Unburned. The significance of it was lost on me.

The letter itself was written on the back of some kind of super-market flier. No fancy-pants stationery for Grimes. And it was written with a ballpoint pen that was running out of ink. Some words were imprinted more heavily than others. I could see and hear him shaking the pen impatiently and cursing it out as if it were a human being. Cindy had quite the granddad.

The message – written in a single paragraph – read as follows:

Conrad,

I had the recorder all along. I called Showalter and told him I wanted a hundred thousand for it. It's my turn to have some money in this life. He said all right. But when I showed up for the hand-off at the boat dock somebody fired at me. Showalter. So I hid the recorder and I'm hiding myself. I'm gonna give him one more chance to pay up. I got a call into him now. If I turn up dead you let Cindy know about this letter and the stick match. She'll know where the recorder is.

Grimes

I folded up the letter, shoved it into my jacket pocket and dropped the stick match into my shirt pocket.

Skully said, 'Now you're gonna help me.'

'I am?'

'You're damn right you are. He dragged me into this. I want you to help me kick him out.'

'I guess that makes sense.'

'Then he's your problem, not mine.'

'Let's go get him then.'

'You stayin' at the Royale and all, I figured you'd be some big snooty asshole. I guess maybe I was wrong. At least a little bit.'

It's all relative, isn't it? You stay at the Four Seasons in Chicago, you might get known as a big snooty asshole. But in Danton, at least for folks like Skully, it's the Royale.

He led the way.

The so-called cabins formed a semicircle in a clearing half-hidden by thick pines. The largest of them was four times the size of the others and bore a large sign that read: TOILETS & SHOWER. The closer we got, the clearer the odors from the building struck like poison gas.

There was no evidence of any guests actually residing in this luxury spa. I could hear highway sounds and nightbird sounds and the sounds we made tramping across downed tree branches from past storms, but none of the noises you associate with human beings bedding down for the night.

'You don't have many people staying here, huh?'

'Technically, we're closed. The old lady died a year ago and it took all the money I had to bury her. Don't have the money to pay for the 'lectricity in the cabins – just the house – so people don't want to stay here when they find that out. Plus the stools're kinda backed up. Your buddy Grimes is the first guest we've had in quite a while. He remembered stayin' here when he was a teenager. Brought his girlfriend out here. Only place he could afford. He's hidin' out tonight so he don't mind not havin' lights.' The last remark warranted his old-man laugh.

We reached Cabin Six by following a curving path, and there situated between two smothering pines was another example of life lived large. Cabin Six managed to be more of a shambles than the others I'd seen. The sole window was taped together with a fashionable swipe of duct tape and the door hung on its hinges with a look of desperation.

'He wanted this one. He said he always used it when he was a kid.'

Grimes would have been in high school in the sixties. Maybe the sex was even better back then with the so-called sexual revolution giving teenagers a freedom previous generations could only have fantasized about.

I stared at the cabin, apprehension starting to fill my chest.

Had somebody beaten me here and killed him? 'Let me go in and check on him.'

'No argument from me, Conrad. I got the gun here if you try anything.'

God alone knew what the hell that meant.

I clipped on my flashlight and moved forward.

I saw two small cots, both swaybacked; a three-drawer bureau, a washbasin and a pitcher on top of it; a single straight-backed chair. The metal bucket was presumably used to pee in. This was the best suite in the house.

Grimes lay on the leftward cot beneath a small pile of faded quilts. In the beam of my light his face was a deep red and his open eyes were also tinted red. He had vomited on himself. This stench was actually preferable to the cabin stench.

From the little I knew about medicine I was somewhat sure I was looking at the victim of a heart attack. Cindy would be free of worrying about him now, even if the worrying was the most profound expression of her love for the old man. I forgot about his greed – why the hell not, anyway; I couldn't argue with his contention that he'd worked hard all his life, even fought for his country, and had little to show for it – and allowed myself to feel some compassion for all the good-bad people in the world. Hell, I was one of them.

'Hey, what's goin' on in there?'

By now I was checking his neck, wrist and ankle for any sign of a pulse. I hadn't expected any and there was none.

'He's dead.'

'Aw, shit. That'll be more bad publicity for this place.'

I had to restrain myself from laughing. It was exactly the right and wrong thing to say on a night like this when so much turmoil ruled.

I had an image of the River Cabins public-relations staff sitting around a conference table à la *Mad Men*, wondering how they were going to deal with this tragedy. The place had such a sterling reputation. Unless they acted quickly and wisely the public might start thinking the place was some kind of dive.

The next thing I did, ghoulish as it was, was search him for the recorder.

He had change, car keys and a rosary in his front pockets. In his back ones there was a billfold and a comb.

I searched the room.

I'm not sure how long it took but a few times I wondered why Skully hadn't either come in or started talking to me again. Then I realized he was talking to somebody else. I kept on searching. There weren't that many places to look but I wanted to get to all of them before Skully interrupted me.

I found nothing and Skully didn't interrupt. Now I wanted to find out who he'd been talking to.

'Called an ambulance and the police,' he said.

'I need to leave now.'

But Skully was good for a plot twist. He shoved the gun in my face and said, 'Like hell you'll leave.'

FORTY

S kully was good at doing two things at once.

He not only kept his firearm on me, he yanked a stopwatch out of his pocket and clicked it on.

'All the damn taxes I pay, let's see how long it takes for them to get here.'

And with that he waved his gun at me and said, 'Let's go up front.'

Given my age and relative condition, it shouldn't have been too much trouble to dive for him and grab his weapon while he was falling to the ground. But Skully was Skully, a crazy but wily bastard who would probably be lucky enough to put two bullets in my head while I was trying to knock him over.

He insisted that he follow me this time.

Now that I'd had a few minutes to consider the fact that Grimes was dead and that Showalter would no doubt attempt to put my name on the suspect list, I decided it would be better to stay here and let Showalter confront me.

Skully and I ended up leaning against my car.

He held the stopwatch high so he could see it in the faint moonlight. 'Five minutes and they ain't here yet.'

He'd been giving me updates, of course, starting at three minutes. Did he really expect the police and an ambulance to get here in three minutes?

Interspersed with the minute-by-minute excitement of waiting for the sirens to arrive, Skully went back through the mistakes he'd made by giving Grimes a cabin at all.

'He looked shifty.'

Grimes did not look shifty.

'And he talked like a hood.'

Grimes did not talk like a hood.

'And as soon as I seen him, I knew I'd have trouble.'

Then why the hell did you give him a room? I thought.

Then it was back to the updates.

'You know how long it's been since I called?'

'No, and I don't really give a shit.'

'You would if you paid the taxes I do.'

As irritating as he was, he at least distracted me from the strange sadness for Grimes that kept creeping back.

'I need to make a phone call. I'm going to step over there.'

'I'll be watchin' you. Don't try anything funny.'

A hopeless son of a bitch.

Cindy answered on the second ring. 'Did you find my granddad?'

'I did, Cindy. He died of a heart attack. At least that's what it looks like to me.'

'Where did you find him?'

I went into the whole story. I waited for her to start crying.

'I know he knew how much I loved him.'

'I'm sure he did, Cindy.'

I'd referenced Grimes's letter only once to her. Now I returned to it.

'Why would he leave me a stick match?'

For the first time tears shook her words. 'I don't know, Dev. I—'

She couldn't restrain herself. A few sobs, then more tears.

I glanced over at Skully. He was watching me like a prison guard. I wondered what the old bastard would do if I flipped him off.

Suddenly she'd snuffled up her tears. 'The votive candles.'

'What?'

'I told you he went to Mass three times a week since my grandmother died. He always lit votive candles for her. That was a big thing for him. That's the only tie I can think of to a stick match. St Paul's is an old church. New churches don't use matches anymore.'

'He hid the recorder in the church?'

'Possibly.' Then, 'I want him brought to the Reardon Mortuary. We all get buried out of there. I'll call the morgue. I'm sure there'll be an autopsy. I'll insist on it.'

A police car pulled up. A minute or so after that an ambulance appeared, and a minute after that another police car.

Skully greeted them with a rant about what a bunch of lazy-ass, incompetent, big-government Nazis they were.

I was able to give one of the officers the basic reason they'd been summoned and where they would find the body. One of the officers hadn't made it past Skully so he was still getting the fiery speech. He took it as long as he could and then snapped.

'I got work to do, old man. Now shut the fuck up and help me.'

Skully stuttered and sputtered but then he actually stopped talking.

All but one of the cops went back to Cabin Six along with the ER team. He sat in his car having a conversation with somebody at the station.

I kept waiting for Showalter to appear. Instead I got Wade.

He'd driven out in a recent-vintage tan Chevrolet sedan. His own, I assumed. He was dressed in jeans, a white shirt and a red windbreaker. He walked right up to me.

'I understand we're having some trouble here tonight, Mr Conrad. Finding a body is a pretty miserable experience. I was in Iraq in '05 and had that happen to me a few times. The worst was finding a little kid.'

His gray eyes scanned the area next to Skully's house.

'When I started out in uniform we were always getting complaints about this place. Skully had a few hookers out here. He was quite the boy back then.' Then, 'So if you wouldn't mind, Mr Conrad, why don't you go over everything for me and we'll get that out of the way.'

Karen was certainly right about Wade's style. He would try to ingratiate you into saying the wrong thing. The words would leave your mouth and you'd hear them and then curse yourself for the duration of the prison term you'd just sentenced yourself to.

So I told him.

He watched me carefully as I spoke. As a good detective he knew all the physical signs of lying. I'd learned them in my days as an army investigator. Trouble swallowing, forced smile, sweating, gestures that don't match what's being said, a voice that changes pitch – standard issue for people who have something to hide.

When I finished, he said, 'And your relationship with Grimes was what exactly?'

'I knew him through his granddaughter.'

'I see. And your relationship to her is what, exactly?'

A white TV van lumbered onto the property, bouncing and jerking as it went through a large and deep hole.

Ever since I'd seen Wade step out of his car I'd been thinking about his relationship with Showalter. Wondering if we couldn't strike a deal.

'Detective Wade, I'm going to say something here that could get me in trouble if you didn't go along with it.'

'You could always call me "Matt." And how would this get you in trouble?'

'Because if you say no to it, it might look as if I'd tried to coerce you into something.'

He raised his head slightly. Rain clouds sped across the three-quarter moon. The smell of impending rain was a relief from the stench of River Cabins.

'I don't have any idea of what you're talking about, but I guess all we can do is find out, right?' He was watching me again as he spoke. He seemed as curious as I'd hoped he would be.

'We don't have a lot of time here, Detective Wade. So I'm going to lay it out.'

'You're stalling.'

'You're right. Karen Foster told me about you and Showalter. How you'd hoped to be chief instead of him.'

'I guess that's not any secret.'

'I can hand him over to you if you'll help me.'

'The recorder?'

'You know about the recorder?'

'The chief doesn't have the most discreet secretary in the city. She says he's been muttering about a recorder the last few days. He's had more than a few meetings with his little group and she hears the word "recorder" through his door constantly.' Then, 'By the way, he's on his way here now. He was the one who called me at home. He's coming from the casino.'

'Do you have any idea what's on this recorder, Detective Wade?'

'No idea at all. But I'm sure as hell curious.'

'Dave Fletcher made a recording before he died. He talked about the things he and Showalter's group have done. I hope he admitted that he fired the shots at Congresswoman Bradshaw and I hope he named all of the men in that group.'

'Well, now I know why *you're* involved in this – Congresswoman Bradshaw. And I know why Showalter's been going crazy. So do you know where the recorder is?'

'No, I don't. But I think I finally know where it might be.'

'So why not get it?'

'I need your help.'

He was interested. Definitely. He kept glancing at the highway.

'What would I need to do?'

'Figure out a way to get me to St Paul's. He'll have me followed for sure.'

'And you'd turn the recorder over to me?'

'After I've listened to it.'

'You're sure it's there?'

'There's only one way to find out.'

'I've waited a long time to get Showalter.'

'So has Karen Foster.'

'I don't know her very well but she's smart as hell and a real professional. I hope she makes it.'

'I'm assuming Showalter had something to do with what happened to her.'

We both saw the new black Lincoln sweep onto the grounds.

He spoke quickly. 'That's Showalter. He'll want somebody to tail you. I'll tell him I'll do it.'

Another unmarked car pulled up next to the Lincoln. A heavy man in a red turtleneck and a black leather coat.

'What the hell's going on here, Conrad?'

Showalter carried heavy scents of liquor and killer cologne. He was back in the Marines again. In charge. Chewing out a suspicious subordinate.

'Skully called me and asked me to come out here.'

'What's he told you so far, Wade?'

'That Grimes had a heart attack.'

'You're an MD now, are you, Conrad?'

'There are certain signs. I could be wrong.'

'No shit you could be wrong.'

I could see him holding court at a bar, meaner the drunker he got and more and more certain of his opinions.

'Now you and I are going back to that cabin and you're going to tell me what happened or I'm going to throw your ass in jail.'

FORTY-ONE

B y the time Showalter seemed about to wrap up his questions for me – more insults and threats than questions really – reporters had made Cabin Six a real crime scene. Two TV crews were allowed to videotape it from the path. Camera lights gave the time-deformed wood of it the aspect of a horror movie. Something hideous might emerge from it at any moment. Something from the grave, of course.

The smells didn't miss them. A woman from one crew kept saying she was going to 'upchuck' and the man of the other said the whole place smelled like an 'Afghan whorehouse.'

Showalter twice made me walk through everything I'd done when I arrived here. Skully was with us most of the time. I'd say something and Skully would comment as to its veracity. One time Showalter said to Skully, 'Did Conrad have time enough to smother him when he was inside?'

'Hell, yes. He was sure pissed off enough when he got here. Grimes was probably three-quarter dead anyway. Wouldn'ta taken much for Conrad to finish him. And when I took a peek inside I saw him goin' through the dead guy's pockets.'

Showalter's body lurched. Between the booze and his urgency to find the recorder, restraint was difficult to come by. 'Did he find anything?'

'I don't think so.'

'Look, you stupid bastard. I want a yes or no answer.'

'Well, I couldn't see everything exactly but I'd have to say no.'

Hurt, not anger, was in Skully's voice. He'd been cooperating with Showalter. He had to wonder why the man had turned on him.

Showalter's breath came in a blast now. Despite the chill, he was sweating. He must have realized how undone he'd sounded.

'I'm sorry, Skully. It's been a long night.'

'That's all right.'

But Skully still sounded hurt.

To me, he said, 'Your friend Edelstein still in town?'

'Yeah, why?'

'The ME said she could have an autopsy for us in twenty hours if we're lucky.'

The medical examiner, a middle-aged woman who carried a black medical bag and a pink umbrella, had spent her time in Cabin Six. Even though she must have been accustomed to working with corpses in various stages of decomposition, apparently the combination of the body and the vile condition of the cabin forced her to duck outside every few minutes and take in deep and grateful lungs full of relatively fresh air. When she'd finished, she'd taken Showalter aside to talk to him. She spoke so softly I didn't catch a single word.

But an autopsy in twenty hours was not going to be easy, and if she felt she needed a toxicology report (which in this case would be prudent, as one of our former presidents liked to say) we were talking weeks.

'I should throw your ass in jail until we get that autopsy, but I don't want to waste my time hassling with Edelstein about bail.'

And if you threw me in jail, you wouldn't have any way to follow me.

'I'm free to go?'

'You shouldn't be, but you are. I'm calling your hotel at seven in the morning and you'd damned well better be there.'

'I'll be sleeping.'

He waved me away with his right hand and with his left jerked a cell phone from his jacket pocket.

Skully not only sounded hurt, he looked hurt. Showalter moved away enough with his phone for me to be able to say, 'Don't worry, Skully. He treats everybody like shit.'

But the hurt remained in those time-worn eyes.

There was even more press up by the highway. In the paper this would be page four at best. If tomorrow's six o'clock news was story-hungry enough it would be story three or four.

Wade sat in his car with the door open, facing me. He was a man who knew how to relax. He waggled his cell phone at me. 'I got the job.'

All I did was nod and walk on past to my own car.

The burly detective who'd arrived just after Showalter was talking to a reporter. He watched me as I climbed inside and started the car. Then he went back to talking.

FORTY-TWO

Long, long ago, I'd been an altar boy.

The Stations of the Cross on both walls, the statues of the Virgin and Jesus on opposite sides of the altar, the altar itself where nothing less than the Body of Christ was said to reside in the form of small thin wafers of bread, the pulpit from which the teachings of the church were spoken to us every weekend . . . and the sensual aspects of the altar, the scents of wine and burning candles and on occasion the sweet, almost hallucinogenic, aroma of heavy incense . . . all this made me feel devout as I served in my pretend-priest costume of white surplice and black cassock . . .

As I entered St Paul's now I felt a melancholy usually reserved for lost loves. I don't recall exactly when I fell out of love with the man-made rules emanating from the Vatican . . . But I did. Maybe sometime in tenth grade or so.

St Paul's was so old it smelled of dampness. As I put my hand on the back pew it wobbled. The rubber runner separating the nave was worn so thin there were holes in it. The Stations of the Cross were faded paintings, and even from here I could see how worn the carpeting around the communion rail was.

At one time this had probably been a prosperous working-class church. But five presidents and numerous Congresses had seen fit to ship the bulk of good working-class jobs abroad, so as the parishioners suffered, so did the church.

Many votive candles were now battery operated. You got the glow but you didn't get the mess. I knew this because an uncle of mine complained every Thanksgiving about how the church had given in to the atheists. That may make sense to you. It never has to me.

St Paul's votive candles were the real thing – six slanted rows of them flickering now in greens and yellows and reds on a gold-painted metal stand that was shedding its skin. Over the stand, at a slight distance, loomed a welcoming statue of Jesus.

Behind me I heard the heavy doors at the front of the church open. I turned to see Wade rushing up the aisle.

'I got waylaid by a traffic accident. Had to take the long way around. So what do we do?'

I took the match from my shirt pocket and explained its significance. 'I assume if he hid it, it's somewhere around here. We may as well start looking under the candles themselves.'

I walked over to the faux-golden stand, dropped to one knee and began feeling the metal underneath the candles. I pictured a recorder you could put in your pocket. It had to be at least large enough to be prominent under the bottom of the stand. The metal was hot below the candles. Hot and flat.

'Anything?' Wade asked.

'Nope.'

'I'll start looking around by the statue. Maybe he hid it behind it.'

'Maybe.'

I should have stood up and joined Wade in searching the general area, but I decided to make one more pass on the underside again.

Hot and flat.

Then I felt something smooth I'd missed before because it was tucked up in a corner. I ripped it down and examined it.

'Is that a piece of tape?'

'Yeah. Grimes must have taped the recorder up there but the tape got warm and it fell down.'

'Then where's the recorder?'

A heavy door opened on the side of the large stone building. Footsteps. A person out of breath. Wade and I just watched each other.

This was the night for old men. Grimes, Skully and now a bald, hefty priest who had to be as old as Skully. He wore the black shirt and Roman collar of his calling. He also wore faded blue jeans.

'Good evening, gentlemen. I'm Father Niles. My bedroom window is right above this side of the church in the rectory so I can hear people in here talking. I just came over to see if there was anything I could do to help. Are you men in any kind of trouble?'

All those years of hearing confessions. He would be practically psychic at reading faces and voices. I'm sure both our body language and our expressions indicated that we were troubled.

'I'm Detective Wade, Father.'

'A detective – Lord, I hope none of our people are in trouble.'

'No, Father. Nothing like that.'

Father Niles's eyes fixed on mine.

'I'm Dev Conrad. I'm the campaign manager for Congresswoman Bradshaw.'

'Oh, well, there are a lot of things I like about her, but I can't vote for her because of abortion.'

He shook my hand anyway.

'Father, we're here because of Frank Grimes,' I said.

'Frank? He's a good man. Especially since his wife died. His faith really returned to him. I hope everything's all right.'

'I'm afraid it isn't, Father. Frank died earlier tonight of a heart attack.'

'Oh, Lord. Poor Frank. He was so confused lately. I said a lot of prayers for him. I'll miss him but I know he's with his wife again now. He missed her so much.'

'Father, you said he was confused lately. He sent me a letter about leaving something for me here at the church. I think the two things may be connected.'

The priest paused, then glanced away. He bit on his lower lip, thinking about things.

'Do you know his granddaughter, Cindy, Mr Conrad?'

'Yes, I do, Father.'

'Well, before I say any more I think I'd better talk to her. And it's too late now to call her. We'd better put this off until morning.'

'No it's not, Father. She's one of the reasons we're here. I can get her on the phone right now and she'll talk to you.'

'At this time of night?'

'Yes, Father. At this time of night.'

I didn't wait. I punched in my speed dial. Her line rang three times. My words came out in one long sentence.

'Cindy, it's Dev. We're at the church here and Father Niles needs to talk to you so please tell him it's all right to help us – here's Father Niles.'

After some reluctance he took my cell phone and said, 'Cindy, it's Father Niles. I'm sorry about this late hour. I'll say the six o'clock Mass for Frank. I'm so sorry about your loss, Cindy.'

I don't suppose they talked much longer than two or three minutes but it seemed interminable. He wanted our identities verified – she couldn't help him with Detective Wade – and our relationship to her grandfather clarified. And then he said, 'Should I tell them everything?'

As he answered his gaze went from me to Wade and back to me again. 'I'll be praying for you and Frank both, Cindy. Good night.' He handed the phone back to me.

'Thanks, Cindy. I'll talk to you later.'

'I just want this to be over, Dev. It sounds as if Father Niles can help you.'

'I sure hope so.'

When the phone was back in my pocket, I said, 'Father, we think Frank taped something underneath the votive candles.'

For the first time, he smiled. He wore dentures.

'Frank didn't tell me where he was going to put it. If he had, I would have told him that the tape might get warm and not hold it. I found it earlier tonight. It's one of those modern things. I wasn't even sure what it was at first. I have a niece who likes to tell me her daughter knows more about this kind of thing than I do. Anyway, I was walking through the church tonight – we leave things open twenty-four hours because we have so many troubled parishioners now and I like to just walk through here in the evening hours – and I found it under the votive lights. As I said, at first I didn't know what it was. I called Frank's place but didn't get any answer.'

'Do you have it now?'

'Yes, I do. It's in a desk in my office at the rectory.'

'Would you get it for us please, Father?'

The smile again. 'You two look as excited as little boys.'

'We'd really appreciate your help, Father.'

'I'll be right back, gentlemen. I just need a few minutes.'

We watched the priest make his slow way to the door and then disappear. Then he was only hollow footsteps on the bare concrete. The side door opened. That should have been followed by the thud of the heavy door closing.

But there was no thud.

Wade noticed it, too. 'Did you hear the door close?'

'No.'

Then came muffled voices. Two pairs of footsteps scraping on the concrete steps.

Showalter towered over Father Niles as he followed the old priest into the church. I wondered if the priest had noticed that Showalter held his Glock low against his leg.

'This must be the night for visitors,' Father Niles said in the tone he probably used when the parish had a party in the basement.

'Father Niles has been nice enough to offer to get me the recorder,' Showalter said. 'But he wanted to make sure that it was all right with you two first. The Father here is a very careful man. But I told him you wouldn't have any objections.'

'I know you talked to Cindy, Mr Conrad. I just wanted to make sure you knew the chief was here.' Again the party voice. 'Can't imagine why it wouldn't be all right. Him being the chief and all.'

'It's fine, Father. Feel free to go get it.'

'I'll be right back then, Chief.'

Like most people, the priest was impressed with rank. Play to the one with the most stripes on his arm. Or the biggest badge.

The three of us stood about five feet apart, listening to Father Niles depart. Showalter showed no signs of drink now. He wore a comfortable, superior smile.

Wade said, 'You followed me.'

'You and Conrad looked too friendly when I pulled into River Cabins. I thought it was a good idea. And by the way, once I get the recorder, I'll be expecting your resignation, Wade.'

'Karen Foster resigned this afternoon. You going to take care of him the way you did her?'

'You're one aggravating son of a bitch, you know that, Conrad? You keep making accusations you can't prove and I'm sick of it.'

'If Karen regains consciousness you're done, Showalter.'

'A woman who created a fake identity for herself and then undermined the entire police force? That'll be another tough sell.'

'Real tough,' Wade said. 'You've got enemies who won't believe anything you say.'

I was glad Wade had taken over the conversation because I needed to think through how I was going to attack Showalter if he gave me the chance. I knew better than to try to get to my Glock. He'd shoot me.

The only hope was to distract him. And right now there was only one way to do it that I knew of.

Wade said, 'You're smiling, Showalter, but you're coming apart. You've got that stress tic in your right eye.'

The sociopathic smile. 'It won't work, Wade. I'm under stress and I can feel the tic but that hardly means I'm coming apart. I used to have a colonel who liked to play mind games like that. He always thought he was tougher than everybody else – superior – and he'd try and make you nervous by playing his games. You know what happened to him? He ate a .38 the night he caught his missus blowing a young lieutenant. I guess he wasn't as tough as he thought. And you aren't either, Wade, so you might as well knock off the bullshit.'

Then I heard the sound I'd been waiting for: Father Niles coming back into the church.

I shouted: 'Don't come in here, Father. Showalter's going to kill both of us!'

'What did you say?' Father Niles tried to shout but his voice was weak.

'Shut your fucking mouth!'

Now it was Wade's turn. 'He's going to kill us, Father! Stay away! We don't want you to get shot!'

His slow footsteps worked slowly up the concrete steps. 'He's going to kill you, you say?'

'You bastard!' Showalter lurched forward as he said this. We'd managed, as I'd hoped, to confuse him for a moment. Now he couldn't afford to shoot us. We'd warned the priest. Showalter would have no way of defending our deaths with the priest as our witness.

'I'm coming up there to see what's going on,' Father Niles said.

Showalter was close enough to try to slam his Glock into my skull, but I ducked under his move and brought my knee up between his legs.

There was a primordial shriek as the pain in his groin began to register. But even so he managed to twist the Glock back into the firing position. A shot fired in rage, it ripped into one of the Stations of the Cross across the nave.

That was when Wade ran three or four steps and launched himself onto Showalter's back. He rode piggyback, using his hands to blind Showalter momentarily. I wrenched his gun hand until I simply slipped the Glock from his grasp. But then Showalter, carrying Wade, slammed into me and knocked the Glock I was carrying – Showalter's Glock – to the floor.

Father Niles was in the doorway now. 'Somebody fired a gun in church! This is terrible.'

That was when Showalter backed up and managed to ram Wade into me. It was an effective move. Both Wade and I staggered backward. I tried to stay on my feet but I stumbled as I moved forward, and took both of us to the floor.

That was when the shots came.

I can't say that I actually saw it. The bullet probably entered the top of Showalter's mouth just before I managed to put both my hands flat on the floor and start pushing myself up.

And then I heard moaning behind me. Wade was on the floor. He'd been shot in the shoulder.

Through gritted teeth, he said, 'Check on Showalter. Get the recorder.'

Father Niles cried out, then began praying. They were just holy words and phrases. I think in that instant he was trying to exorcise all three of us who remained alive. And his church. After what had just happened the church itself needed to cast out its demons.

Showalter lay on his back, his right hand still holding the gun he'd used to take his own life. There was such a mixture of blood and bone and tissue on the floor behind him I wondered if it could ever be cleansed away.

The old priest knelt next to the body and prayed frantically, crossing himself numerous times as he did so.

I hoped he had a few prayers left over for the rest of us.

FORTY-THREE

If you've followed the career of one Richard M. Nixon, then the name Rose Mary Woods will be familiar to you. She was, of course, his secretary and she was, of course, the woman who 'accidentally' erased a section of tape. Conventional wisdom is that the tape contained things that would have damaged his presidency even more.

My father the political consultant loved telling Watergate tales. He told them right up to his death, several years after the fact. He especially loved the Rose Mary Woods story – how it was impossible to have 'accidentally' erased it the way she said she had and how she was loyal to the point of facing prison for the villainous Dick Nixon (who'd actually done a number of very good things for our country, damn his paranoid hide). I'm no different. I love Watergate stories. And no matter how old I get, Rose Mary Woods will always make me smile in that superior way.

Or I should say I found Rose Mary amusing until I got the digital recorder back to my office after Showalter took his own life and Detective Wade went into the hospital with a serious wound between his shoulder and his heart, leaving me with the recorder overnight.

I was still working in my office when the staff started trooping in with coffee and questions about the shootout at the church. Because I was exhausted I didn't realize that their questions would be joined by dozens and dozens more when the press started questioning me during the next three days, right up to the night of the final debate.

I had transferred the recording to my computer and gone to work on it. A good deal of it was Dave's rambling about the 'New America' he and his cohorts were going to found. It was only toward the end that he spent a drunken, rambling eight minutes talking about Showalter and his group. The chief had indeed run his old scam. His group – and Dave named all the men involved – had robbed four banks for him out of state and turned the funds over to him for safekeeping. There was plenty on the tape to convict the cops who'd been in the group. His remorse for being part of the staged shooting came at the very end. And then he revealed who'd helped him with the staged shooting. I just sat there, stunned. At first I tried to reject the name on the tape, but why would Dave have lied? This was a name that would destroy a number of people. It was there that I went all Rose Mary Woods. I edited it out entirely and permanently.

When Abby came in I told her about the recording and asked her to deliver the copy I'd made to Wade's office. Then we devised between us how the contents of the recording, which had four references to the friendship between Showalter and Dorsey, would be leaked to the press in time for the debate tonight.

Before I left the office I checked on the condition of both Karen

Foster, who was conscious now, and Matt Wade, who had just talked to the press from his hospital bed. The mayor had been there and had referred to him as 'Police Chief Wade' several times.

I hung out the DO NOT DISTURB sign and crashed for seven straight hours.

The press was up for a lynching that night.

They had tightened the noose but not dropped the trapdoor with Jess about the staged shooting. Frustrated that they hadn't gotten a clean kill with her they were – God bless 'em – going to take out their fury on Dorsey.

In between questions about the economy, pay for teachers, prayer in school, foreign policy and economic recovery, the four press representatives pounded him with inquisitional queries about his relationship with Showalter. Abby had leaked just the right allegations so it would be easy to assume that Showalter had been behind the fake shooting. Among many, many other high crimes.

Dorsey stammered, sputtered, exploded and sweated. By the end of the debate he looked like he'd just run through a car wash. He would not shake hands with Jess afterward, at which time his handlers probably raced to the nearest bar. Not what you'd call a wise choice on Dorsey's part.

I had to wonder if he'd provide the press with a second suicide.

The next night there were two stretch limos in front of Jess's magnificent home.

One belonged to our governor and the other to our senator. When I say 'our,' I mean our party.

There was a six-piece band, bright, quick alcohol bearers to make sure your intake would set records, a male television personality from Chicago who had been famous when I was a kid, at least three unattached thirty-something women who took at least a vague shine to me because I, too, was unattached, and all our office staff.

I gave up counting the number of toasts that were made when we sat around a mahogany table long enough to land a jet fighter on. Even Cory Tucker, sitting next to his very attractive girlfriend, made a toast. This was the pre-victory victory party, but after our campaign had been absolved of all suspicion in the staged shooting incident, plus Dorsey's psycho performance last night, the only thing that could stop us from winning was if either Jess or Ted admitted to keeping small children caged in the basement.

Just before the food came – catered seafood, chicken, pork and beef entrées, and damned good at that – Ted pinged his glass with his fork and stood up. Then he reached down and took Jess's hand.

To the assembled, he said, 'Some of you may have heard the dirty rumor that the love of my life and I are getting a divorce. Speaking for both of us, I can tell you that's a filthy lie!'

There was applause, tears and more applause. They would return to their God-given right as a Washington power couple.

I drank with Katherine, then with one of the unescorted women, then decided that if I could sneak out of here sober enough I could go back to my hotel room and call my daughter. And then I could get up with no hangover in the morning and spend three or four hours in Karen's hospital room since she was conscious now.

Mike Edelstein halted the band mid-tune to lead those sober enough to hoist their glasses in what had to be the hundredth toast. It was while I was supporting my glass in the air that I saw my person of interest slip out to the small patio. Hoping we'd be alone, I followed.

The big prairie moon lent the patio a proper mood of melancholy. Just right for what I was about to say.

'Oh, Dev. I didn't hear you come out here.'

'I just needed to talk to you a little bit.'

He had good radar. That handsome Bradshaw face of his clenched and then he turned his back to me. Two hundred yards or so away from here you could see the river. It was moonlit and tranquil, and on the far shore you could see a few campfires despite the chill. 'I guess you figured it out, huh?'

'Yeah.'

He faced me again. 'But the news makes it sound as if Showalter was behind it.'

'That was my intention.'

'But why? I'm the guilty one.'

'I'm hoping you have a reason for doing it that's so good I won't feel guilty about covering for you.'

'God, this is when I really need a drink.'

'Don't even joke about that, Joel.' Given his history of alcoholism I was afraid he might be half-serious.

'I wish I at least had a smoke.' He folded his hands and stared down at them. He didn't speak for a time.

Far downriver, I could hear motorboats.

'What did it was how they treated Katherine when she was sick. They let the public know about it because it was good press – the poor congresswoman and all that bullshit – but if it hadn't been for Nan and me, Katherine would've been alone most of the time.' He took his hands apart, then raised his head. 'They just got worse and worse and worse over the years. With her, I mean. There's no room for anybody but them. For Katherine's sake I decided to take away the only thing that mattered to them.'

'Her Congressional seat.'

'Yes.'

'You hired Dave Fletcher to do the fake shooting, knowing that the press would know it was a fake almost immediately.'

'And she'd lose. And both Jess and my dear brother wouldn't be the superstars they think they are. God, what a word. "Superstars." It almost gags me to say it. But that's how they look at themselves.'

'A lot of them do.'

'"A lot of them?"'

'Politicians. And it's both sides of the aisle. They become megalomaniacs.'

The smile was bleak. 'I guess you'd know. You've worked with enough of them.'

'As long as they generally vote the right way. That's all I ask for. As people – well, you can go into a factory or supermarket and pick twenty people at random and you'll find twenty better people than you'll find at random in Congress.'

'Hey, there you are!'

Ted was drunk. His champagne glass was held at a sixty-degree angle.

'We're sort of talking here, Ted,' I said.

'Well, fucking excuse me. You're such a fucking superior being you forget I write your check every month.'

'Actually, Jess does, Ted,' Joel said.

I could not have predicted his reaction. The arrogant, drunken, angry Ted Bradshaw said: 'We're supposed to be brothers. Why would you say something like that to me?' He teetered as he said this and champagne ran from his tilted glass like a rich boy's piss. I thought he was going to cry.

'You say stuff like that all the time to me, Ted.'

But then Jess was in the doorway, saying, 'C'mon Ted, the governor and his wife want to say goodbye to us.'

She wisely a) took his glass from his hand, b) pushed her arm through his and c) guided him into the still-going-strong party.

Joel offered a slight smile and shook his head. 'What a couple.'

'Thank God Katherine has always had you.'

'She had me when I was sober, anyway.' He was beating himself up. Then, 'And speaking of sober, this is the kind of thing I never admitted to anybody even when I was drunk, but I'm going to tell you, Dev. And I'm going to trust that you'll never tell anybody else.'

He hit somebody with his car when he was drunk. He had been embezzling campaign funds. He was gay. He'd taken a couple of drinks tonight despite telling me he was sober. What the hell was he going to tell me?

'Katherine's actually my daughter.'

I had to quickly survey all the words in the English language so I'd know what to say. I didn't want to sound shocked because that might hurt his feelings. And I didn't want to sound judgmental in any way because he'd been her real father all along.

'I'm not quite sure why, but that doesn't surprise me.'

'Ted was having one of his flings and Jess was having particular problems with this one so she showed up at my apartment in Georgetown. She was very drunk. And I was pretty drunk myself. It was one of those periods when I was trying to convince myself that I could handle having a few drinks. Anyway, we made love several times that night. Maybe there was a little bit of revenge in it for her but I think that at the time we were both just desperately needy people.

'And two months later she called and said she was pregnant and that it couldn't be Ted's because he hadn't touched her in a while.'

'Ted never suspected?'

'No. He gets sort of crazy when he's having his relationships. As far as I know, he's never suspected. He just assumed that he and Jess slept together during his fling and Katherine was the result.'

'You ever going to tell her?'

'I'm not sure she could handle it.'

'Maybe what you're saying is that you're not sure your brother could handle it.'

Then she was in the doorway – the fragile beauty and the elegant wan presence of her, his daughter, Katherine.

'The band's going to play a slow song, Uncle Joel. You still owe me a dance.'

'You didn't think I was going to forget, did you?'

'No, but I know how much fun it is to talk to Dev. You never want to leave.'

'Wow,' I said. 'I'm sending you a check for that one, Katherine.'

She laughed and held out her slender arm. 'C'mon now, Uncle Joel. Before the song ends.'

'I'm a lucky man,' Joel said as he went to her.

'And she,' I said, 'is a lucky woman.'

FORTY-FOUR

W e won the election by six points.

During the course of the real victory party two weeks later I found out that Katherine was going to work as Joel's assistant, that Abby was on the verge of being engaged, that Mike Edelstein's sudden biopsy for possible prostate cancer revealed that he was fine and that neither Jess nor Ted seemed dismayed in the slightest when I told them I was resigning.

Wade got one of Showalter's dirty cops to admit that Showalter and his buddy Dorsey saw an easy opportunity to take down Jess so they planted the rifle in Cory's trunk. As for Cory, he told me he needed to take a break from politics. I gave him a thousand dollars of Jess's campaign money to enjoy his break.

'Truth be told, Dev,' Ted said as we sat in his den, him playing the hard-nosed politician he was in his dreams, 'I've been talking to a couple of firms and they think Jess needs a redo on some things.'

'But if we get any calls for recommendations, Dev, there'll be nothing but praise for you,' Jess said.

'Hell, not just praise, Dev. Super praise.'

'Wow. Just plain old praise is hard enough to come by. But super praise—'

'That's Dev for you, honey. You try to pay him a compliment and he comes back with a cynical remark. We're gonna miss that, Dev.'

'We're going to miss it a lot,' Jess said.

She'd made herself a stranger to me in the past few days. She was a clone that had programmed me out of her memory.

Ted stood up. 'Well, I'd say it was time for more champagne.'

But it wasn't, of course. Not with them anyway. Not with them.

I got to the hospital in time to spend a full hour with Karen.

She told me that the new Chief Wade had visited her and she'd explained how Showalter had chased her up into the hills and then piled into her car so she'd be driven into the ravine.

Then we talked about what she was going to do in the future. I told her Chicago was a good place to be, especially since this campaign manager she'd said a few nice things about happened to live there, too.

Then I showed her iPhone photos of some of the Chicago apartments I'd been looking at. I needed more space because you just couldn't tell when somebody might want to move in with you.

She smiled that smile of hers and said no, you really never could predict when somebody just might move in with you.

I thought that it was awful nice of her to understand.